7 - ONE ACT PLAYS

7 - ONE ACT PLAYS

A LIFE'S JOURNEY
VOLUME 2

JERRY JOSH KONSKER

ReadersMagnet, LLC

7 - One Act Plays: A Life's Journey Volume 2
Copyright © 2021 by Jerry Josh Konsker

Published in the United States of America
ISBN Paperback: 978-1-954371-83-5
ISBN Hardback: 978-1-955603-32-4
ISBN eBook: 978-1-954371-82-8

All rights reserved. No part of this publication may be reproduced, stored in a retrieval system or transmitted in any way by any means, electronic, mechanical, photocopy, recording or otherwise without the prior permission of the author except as provided by USA copyright law.

ReadersMagnet, LLC
10620 Treena Street, Suite 230 | San Diego, California, 92131 USA
1.619.354.2643 | www.readersmagnet.com

Book design copyright © 2021 by ReadersMagnet, LLC. All rights reserved.
Cover design by Ericka Obando
Interior design by Mary Mae Romero

A Life's Journey
Volume II
7-One Act Plays

Josh Konsker

For Judi

ABOUT THE AUTHOR

My grandfather taught me how to write. We would sit together in his library, reading or writing independently. The soft sound of pages turning rippled through the air. A faint scent of 70-year-old canvas book covers with aging ink and paper wafted through our concentration. Time stood still. I was lost in study, not only in my own project but in observance of my grandfather. He had an effortless dedication to his work. Every time I write I hear him. He challenges me to use the voice that is uniquely my own. Great mentors have a way of teaching us how to find ourselves.

My belief is my grandfather would write to understand the human condition. He wrote what he knew to help himself understand what he knew. The written word can unveil our motivations and the motivations of those around us. Through his endless study and practice, my grandfather found a way to share what he learned. His working catalogue is truly prolific. Theater is his medium of choice and often described as his first love; his passion that connected with his whole self.

To the reader of this collection, consider the human condition. What motivates us to do what we do or say what we say? Writing for theater is unique to other styles of writing because depth and dimension are assumed and inherent to the audience. While reading these plays allow them the space to move, speak and breath as they would on stage. Let them live, as they were intended to.

-Aaron Konsker

The books upon the shelves that decorate the perimeter of my uncle's study in his Florida home contain more than the words of Hemingway and Miller and Shakespeare and Eliot; they speak of the man who read them - of his tragedies, his fortunes, and of his passions elicited from the words marked in ink upon their pages.

Smudges from his sweat and dirt-stained fingertips narrate his stories as a soldier fighting in Korea - of the long nights he spent with a dim flashlight, made dim purposely, one can assume, as the bright, flashing light in the night may have alarmed a scared boy or two with whom he shared a tent.

Torn, dog-eared leaflets from within the seventy-year-old bound books in his robust Hemingway collection chronicle a life filled with musings of romance and loss, ascension and decline, courage and valor and defeat and collapse.

The tears besmirched upon the pages of Eliot's "…Prufrock" recant the times of hundreds of recitings and hundreds of re-readings - most notably of the one spoken to his beloved wife, Judith, upon their first date, whilst sitting beneath a cherry-blossom tree at Sunken Meadow Park, on a hot day in August of 1956.

Spanning close to nine decades, the books that inspired my uncle throughout his life inspire those who knew him, yet having known my uncle, these stories are empowered with more than that which the authors who wrote them may have intended. It was how my uncle spoke of these stories that inspired my love for them; it was how he narrated their words that enabled me to feel them; it was my uncle's musings of language and the spoken word that has served as the catalyst for my enduring fascination with the power they embody.

Jerome 'Josh' Konsker was born in the Bronx, New York on September 22, 1933 to Rose, 24, and Morris Konsker, 27. The eldest of three boys, Jerry, as he had come to be called, attended NYU in 1950, studying under the famed author Arthur Miller for two semesters before enlisting in the army to serve in the Korean War from 1952 to 1953. Having paid witness to combat, his writing altered in its course; the romantic poetry that once decorated his journals, in its stead, transposed the pains of war and the unintelligible world within which he, at one time, struggled to endure. Yet, we beat on, and after marrying his wife of 64 years, earned the title of patriarch to an immediate family bearing three boys, seven grandchildren, and three great-grandchildren. His relationships with his wife, children, brothers, nieces and nephews and grand-nieces and grand-nephews - his relationships with all those fortunate to have known him are his legacy, and their lasting impact are his gift.

It has been through grief that I have learned to appreciate or value this concept: what we bring from those - the dead - with us - the living - is the only thing that keeps them 'alive' in the form with which we have come to understand life in this universe. We are enhanced because we knew them, and we only risk losing their enduring companionship by neglecting their stories - those for which they were part and those of which they shared.

In this book, you will find my uncle's stories. Through his poetry, plays, short stories, chapters to a novel or novella or a project yet to be inspired, he shared a piece of himself to live on forever; thus, it is only fitting that these stories are shared for anyone who wants to listen, for anyone who wants to learn, for anyone who wants to love and to be loved and to know the difference.

My beloved uncle was a man of many, many words. Here are some for you.

-Alyson Konsker-Lorenzo

CONTENTS

About the Author vii

A Door...A Passage 1
In Pursuit Of 45
Troop Ship 81
Jacob 110
A Moveable Light 139
The Stifling 155
New Directions 185

A DOOR...A PASSAGE

A ONE ACT PLAY

By JERRY "JOSH" KONSKER

"We choose a road on which to walk...That road is never to be tread but once in our lives... never allowing us to return to its origin"
**Colonel Father Murphy, Head Chaplain
7th Infantry Division, Korea 1953**

The story of a young man, so consumed by his experiences as a soldier that he becomes part of a personal never-ending war. Can he return to civilian life with his family, love, and creature comforts?

[STAGE SET: A VERY WELL-APPOINTED DRAWING ROOM OF AN ESTATE HOME...WALLS ARE DECORATED WITH OIL PAINTINGS...ONE WALL HAS BOOKCASES HOLDING LEATHER BOUND VOLUMES... THERE IS A SMALL BAR ON THE STAGE LEFT WALL...FOUR GLASS DOORS ON REAR WALL LEADING TO A FLOWER FILLED TERRACE. CUSHIONED CHAIRS THROUGHOUT THE ROOM]

Cast of Characters:

BEATRICE: A handsome woman of 60. Fighting to stave off the effects of age. Mother of Michael and Sam.

ALLYSSIA: Sister of Beatrice 62...tall and slim woman...well put together physically and mentally

SARAH: Longtime friend of Beatrice 60...well dressed but shows her age and is somewhat unnerved in today's atmosphere

BERNARD: Known as Beanie...tall and distinguished and a long time close friend of Beatrice...

LAURA: An attractive though not beautiful woman 33...Sarah's daughter

MICHAEL: Eldest son of the family 35...masculine and athletic....already showing signs of grey.

[AS CURTAIN OPENS: LAURA IS SEATED DOWN TO THE RIGHT...ALYSSIA IS BY THE BAR STANDING... SARAH STANDS DOWN LEFT]

ALLYSSIA: Isn't this silly?...like a party before the party

SARAH: And without all the players....Bea won't celebrate her birthday until her sons have arrived.....they should have been here already

ALLYSSIA: I was sure Michael would be here by now.

SARAH: What a surprise that is....Laura, you've had a crush on him as long as I can remember

LAURA: Well.... Only since I was 6....he was 8...that's when I realized that boys were different than girls....and Michael was very different.

ALLYSSIA: I'm afraid that he is still different....and different in too many ways....I must confess, I'm as anxious as you are....and my crush is even longer than yours dear....although hardly for the same reasons.

SARAH: I believe that Sam is coming with his whole family, isn't he?

ALLYSSIA: Of course....they haven't seen Michael for a long time either....in fact,...the little ones don't know him at all....Michael and Sam were so close as boys, despite how different their personalities were.....Sam, so steady....Michael, well, just kind of all over the place....

LAURA: I just find it so difficult to understand....Michael served six years in the army....three tours in Vietnam....wounded twice, highly decorated.....it's been more than three years since his discharge...why doesn't he come home?

ALLYSSIA: He's working for Time Magazine now as a war correspondent....it seems that's what he wants to do....he's in the Middle East now....there's always a war going on over there.

LAURA: Why does he have to follow wars?... There's so much more for him here.

ALLYSSIA: I wish I could answer that...but Michael has always been difficult to understand....

SARAH: Sam has two children now, doesn't he?

ALLYSSIA: A boy four and a girl two....Michael's never seen them....and since Evelyn works full time also....Sam has become a Mister Mom....

LAURA: That would never happen to Michael

SARAH: True, I can't imagine Michael with an apron on or cleaning a dirty diaper.....

[BEANIE ENTER FOM STAGE LEFT]

ALLYSSIA: Beanie, have you heard anything?

BEANIE: Sam is held up in Chicago....strong winds or something....from Michael though.....nothing.

SARAH: *[in a condescending tone]* Is her lady-ship planning to spend any time with the proletariat, or is she waiting for the prince to come?

BEANIE: She's upstairs resting.....emotionally, this is a very big day for her...Allyssia, you should understand, you're her sister.

ALLYSSIA: *[noticeable tension in her voice]* I may be her sister but I only see her a few times a year....we have tea....I listen to her self-aggrandizing nonsense....and then I get away....You're the one who practically lives here and you're the one who's been sucking up to her for the last twenty five years.....

BEANIE: That's unfair, I------

ALLYSSIA: I'll bet you even get laid as often as I have tea...

SARAH: Stop it Allyssia....Beanie's been a good friend to all of us for a long time now....no one can really explain love, infatuation, or the willingness to subjugate oneself to another

BEANIE: Ladies...it's not right to_____

ALLYSSIA: *[continuing the attack]* Maybe it's the Country Club she put you in, it makes up for all the dead time...There's tennis and golf....a well-stocked bar....and let's not forget all the lonely ladies who need personal fulfillment now and then....you know that game as well as tennis....

LAURA: Cut it out you two old crones...Beanie doesn't warrant your critique. Neither of you have any major accomplishments to speak of. *[To Beanie]* ...Beanie have you heard anything from Michael recently? Doesn't he call or write, anything??

BEANIE: *[RELIEVED TO CHANGE THE SUBJECT]* Actually, very little......we learn more about him from the magazines and papers he works for....and oddly,...this year, two members of his old platoon in Vietnam came looking for him..... it seems that many members of Love Company are trying to get together....a few are still not beyond their ugly memories....they can't cope....into drugs, alcohol and the like.....a group is trying to help them....those veterans said that Michael, who was their platoon officer and a real leader through the worst of it, was especially good with men breaking down....he had a real knack for reaching into people....they were hoping he might be available...

SARAH: He is certainly far from the boy I knew while he was growing up.....

LAURA: *[ALMOST DEFENSIVELY]* He's not a boy....he's a man...and apparently quite a man...but you never knew him as I did...this is no different from growing up...he was always near the top of everything he tried....he played baseball and football in high school and college....he was a top student...everybody was his friend....every girl in school loved him...he flirted with all of them, but he never hurt anybody....the only girl he didn't pay attention to was me.....

SARAH: You were two years younger than Michael, Laura....to him you were baby....a family friend.

LAURA: To him, I may have been a baby....but my hormones didn't think so....

SARAH: *[TRYING TO SMOOTH HER DAUGHTER'S FEELINGS]* Even though,....your relationship was more family than anything else...I have no doubt he recognized you as a lovely and bright young girl and even later as a woman...he simply couldn't get over the kid image....

ALLYSSIA: Now, he's widowed from the woman he married in China...he's single again ....he'll certainly see you as the charming woman you are now.....

LAURA: I hope so...

BEANIE: Okay... I'm going to check if I have any messages from Michael *[HE EXITS]*

SARAH: It looks like we'll be sitting here awhile....open the liquor cabinet Allyssia... if you find cards, we can play gin rummy when Beanie gets back.

7 - ONE ACT PLAYS

[BEATRICE ENTERS AS ALLYSSIA IS SPEAKING]

BEATRICE: If you're going to the cabinet, I'll take sherry...... don't just stand there looking at me...say hello!

ALLYSSIA: I guess tea time will be longer than usual....we're all dying to see Michael....

LAURA: Beatrice, what have you heard from him?....he isn't hurt, is he? I mean, he's running around all those crazy places...I hope he's all right.

BEATRICE: Truth be told, I don't know any more than you do.... but I don't think he's hurt....I made such a fuss about his reaching thirty-five and me sixty, that he reacted....also, I intimated in a few of my letters that I've been ill....

SARAH: That wasn't quite fair.....

BEATRICE: Fair be damned....I only care about seeing my son...I must have him here and to his senses before he gets killed somewhere chasing rainbows...., I tell you, every time a stranger comes to the door, I fear that he's bringing some terrible news of Michael...

BEANIE: *[ENTERING]* Nothing yet from Michael *[SEEING BEATRICE]* Oh Bea, you made it down....good for you....there was word from Samuel....There'll be no flights out of Chicago till morning.....sends his regrets....says, enjoy the party....he'll come with family next weekend.....

ALLYSSIA: How nice.....can I come two weeks in a row sis? To see the children of course....

BEATRICE: Don't be silly....or sarcastic...you know you're welcome whenever you please....you have your own room....

ALLYSSIA: All right dear sister....truce....this is an important day for you......in fact, for all of us....we'll put discordant thoughts aside.....

BEATRICE: Thank you........

SARAH: We should also talk about Sam....how, the devil, are he and his family? We haven't seen them for years....not since the birth of little Jessica.

BEATRICE: They've been here a few times.....for holidays Chicago satisfies Samuel very well....and he has enough responsibilities in the mid-west....he needn't take on any more than that....

ALLYSSIA: Is he satisfied?....or is it that you're satisfied?.....

BEATRICE: We both are....one should not rise above their ability.....

ALLYSSIA Ability or nobility?

BEATRICE: And what sister is that supposed to mean?

ALLYSSIA: That the second son can't be king!!!

BEATRICE: Second sons seldom become kings....and why are we talking about kings?

ALLYSSIA: Of course we're talking about kings....she's holding the post, as Queens would....for her first son, Michael, to became the king of Crane's....

BEATRICE: Why shouldn't I?.....Crane's is a multibillion dollar enterprise,...and it will take someone like Michael to control it......

ALLYSSIA: That's horse feathers....Crane's done very well for the family since Jacob died twenty nine years ago....as CEO, you're only a figurehead....Michael would be like the King of England....all pomp and no circumstance...I don't think Michael could do that.

BEATRICE: Michael can do anything he sets his mind to....he's a born leader....we've all seen that....

ALLYSSIA: Yes he is....but as a leader, he must lead....and he must choose his own directions....

BEATRICE: We'll see about that, won't we?

LAURA: *[UPSET BY THE DIRECTION OF THE DIALOGUE]* But, even if Michael chooses his own direction.... and he will.....why can't it be close to home,... to us?

SARAH: Laura....why are you so upset?

LAURA: Because Michael can't be happy with what he's doing.... the wars....the depravity...the filth...and most of all.....the danger....

SARAH: It's his choice...the things he's done...

LAURA: He's done enough!!

ALLYSSIA: Laura, maybe he will want to stay...and maybe he will want to stay with you....I'd be happy to see that...

LAURA: *[SOMEWHAT CONTRITE]* I'm sorry, I didn't mean to explode like that...but like I said...I still have a crush....a lot more than a crush...and I would help him, I would be his partner.....

BEATRICE: I see that everyone has their own agenda....shall we simply split my Michael up?

SARAH: That's it....your Michael...just as you tried to control Jacob...you'll push Michael away too.....

BEATRICE: Push Jacob? I didn't push Jacob...he just floated....and he floated to you, didn't he Sarah?

SARAH: You don't understand, I------

BEATRICE: I'm afraid I understand very well....you didn't like your own marriage, so you did the one thing you couldn't do in college ...you stole my date....

SARAH: You are such a control freak.....Jacob------

BEATRICE: Do you think I don't know about Jacob and you.....It only ended because he died.....

SARAH: Yes and left you the queen....

BEATRICE: A queen with two sons.....and maybe a half daughter.....Perhaps we should check Laura's blood....Laura, you very well be Michael and Samuel's half sister.....

7 - ONE ACT PLAYS

LAURA: What are you saying?----

ALLYSSIA: That's it stop....all of you... this is not the way.... Laura, don't listen to them

LAURA: But my mother....Mr. Crane.... I don't remember?

ALLYSSIA: You can't remember dear.....you were too young.... Jacob Crane was more of a man than his wife would ever let him be.....so he found other solace....and other diversion....

LAURA: But my father?

ALLYSSIA: Your father was a very sick man.....even though he was young....and then he died shortly before you were born......

SARAH: Laura.....please try to understand------

LAURA: Understand what?....that I am thirty three years old and I don't know who I am?...That I may be in love with my brother?... What a kick in the ass that is....I'm going out to the garden....you can all decide what my future should be...perhaps you'll even be thoughtful enough to tell me?...[SHE EXITS}

SARAH: *[to Beatrice]* ...You bitch.... Why did you have to do that?

BEATRICE: And why did you have to screw with my husband?.... weren't you happy enough that I had a bad marriage?

SARAH: Bad? ....no....you had what you wanted....two sons and a lot of money

ALLYSSIA: Money helps a lot of things Sarah....if Beatrice is correct, I suggest you go out and have a long talk with your daughter.....

SARAH: Okay...okay....you're right Alyss....I better go out....

[SHE EXITS LEAVING ALLYSSIA AND BEATRICE ALONE]

ALLYSSIA: [*looking slowly at Beatrice*] ...And then there were none... that's the last of your friends Bea......

BEATRICE Sarah deserved to be called out.... I've waited years for the right opportunity....she took my husband and she used him....

ALLYSSIA You're delusional...she didn't take him...you gave him to her...and you really didn't care at the time....as long as he left you alone...you ignored him.. you horsed around at the county club with a progression of Beanies....and now you have your own Beanie, full time.....

BEATRICE What's wrong with Beanie.

ALLYSSIA: Nothing...really...he's a nice man...of course, at his age he can't make very much money as a tennis pro any longer... he's beholden to you...right under your thumb......

BEATRICE: **[DEFENSIVELY]**   He's a lot more than you realize!!

ALLYSSIA: I hope so...for your sake....because now you can live out your days in this ivory tower...one of your own making....

7 - ONE ACT PLAYS

Sarah won't return...nor will Laura...Samuel will show minimal allegiance....I'll come occasionally, like I do now...if I've nothing better to do...and I doubt if you will hold Michael......

BEATRICE: We'll see....Michael is still mine...

ALLYSSIA: No...he stopped being yours the day he put on a uniform...The lieutenant bars said..."TODAY I AM MY OWN MAN"

BEATRICE: Well, I have kept his place in this family alive....

ALLYSSIA Do you know anymore? Do you read his letters? Follow his career? Have you ever met the woman he married?

BEATRICE I wouldn't allow her here...she was a tramp...a camp follower.......I wouldn't even write him when she was killed......

ALLYSSIA She was far from a tramp....she was a photographer... and a good one...internationally known....

BEATRICE: Well, he can remarry here....a nice normal woman...

ALLYSSIA Like Laura?

BEATRICE: Yes....like Laura....!!

ALLYSSIA: But you certainly sabotaged that one,...didn't you?

BEATRICE She'll get over it fast enough...she wants Michael....

ALLYSSIA But, as you said, she could be Jacob's-----

BEATRICE She could be....so what?

ALLYSSIA God…you are so blind when you want to be….she could have been the glue you needed to keep him here…now she can only be Michael's confusion

BEATRICE *[ALMOST LIKE A SCHOOL CHILD]*…and what makes you so smart about children? …you've never had any of you own!

ALLYSSIA Correct….but that could be my advantage….I can be objective and subjective at the same time….maybe not as a mother….but very close to it…and I certainly love Michael as I would my own….

BEATRICE So, you would like to take my child away from me?

ALLYSSIA Don't be stupid….I can't take what is already away…

BEATRICE You would have him abandon his family duty….. his responsibilities?

ALLYSSIA Oh Bea,…those things exist only in your mind…not his….never will they….Bea…you have never understood him…and now, I doubt if he will understand himself.

[THE LIGHTS DIM ON STAGE…BRING IN A GARDEN BENCH…AS THE LIGHTS COME UP, SARAH IS SEATED ON THE BENCH…LAURA STANDS NEARBY]

LAURA Explain to me mother….why, at the age of thirty three, my life is turned upside down by that woman?

SARAH What she implied was a nasty insinuation…she only wanted to hurt me….not you

LAURA Somehow, she missed her mark....or maybe she hit her mark...but the arrow had to pass through me to get to you?

SARAH There are many things, dear. Of which you are not aware....one must try to understand----------

LAURA That's rather obvious....like, who my father may be....why is there even a question?

SARAH: Laura, sit for a moment [LAURA SITS ON THE SAME BENCH WITH Sarah, BUT AS FAR AWAY AS POSSIBLE]...Let me try to explain.....this story must go all the way to high school...Beatrice and I were close friends....but she was very aggressive, and I was the passive member of the duo...it continued through college.

LAURA: And-----

SARAH In our junior year, I met Jacob Crane....It was in philosophy class....I remember it so well....Jacob was a star in that course....in fact, Jacob was a star in every course he took.....we, somehow hit it off....he was a tall handsome man. Very smart and, of course, very wealthy....I made the mistake of introducing him to Beatrice....she went after him in a way that I never could...he was hardly left out of her sight...." The perfect catch "....handsome, smart, and wealthy.....the lifestyle and the beautiful children she longed for....

LAURA: You could have stopped her.....

SARAH I couldn't....they married right after graduation.......she got the estate...and then she got Michael and Samuel.......but she didn't quite get the lifestyle she wanted...... "fast and furious"..... this wasn't Jacob....their marriage became in name only......

LAURA So he came crawling back to you....you were married.....

SARAH Yes, I was married...and I loved Seymour....the man you've always known as your father....but shortly after our wedding, he became very sick and very weak....he could hardly work....I was the breadwinner...but I never deserted him

LAURA And Jacob satisfied your sex life?

SARAH Oh no....at least not at first....we just became friends.... Jacob would take me to the theater or the opera...Seymour knew of our friendship....he knew Jacob....but eventually, we became physical too.....

LAURA Then you became pregnant....

SARAH Yeas...I became pregnant...and to this day, I'm not certain who your father is....they were both very good men...

LAURA Is that supposed to make me feel better?

SARAH: Let me finish....Seymour died when you were a year and a half old....that's why you don't remember him....Jacob had a heart attack and passed when you were five...I'd lost both men I loved....but I had you...

LAURA You managed to raise me very comfortably on a teacher's salary...

SARAH Jacob secretly established a trust fund for you and me... that is why my salary served us so well....

LAURA Well...what do I do now? How do I find out? Blood tests? I would need blood from Michael or Samuel...and even then, it may not be conclusive...

SARAH Laura, you look like Seymour....he was a handsome man too..tall, yourself this is so....and live with it......

LAURA And this modern soap story is supposed to satisfy me.? Let's analyze the situation....my mother had a sick husband... "for better or worse" in the marriage contract, was put on the back burner....that's because she had an old boyfriend in the wings...... and she couldn't keep her legs closed....

SARAH Laura, please!!

LAURA So,...now I have a lovely choice between two handsome fathers...one rich and one poor....the only problem is that I've always been drawn to the rich man's son that does so pose a dilemma, doesn't it....What should I tell Michael? I don't want you to fall in love with me....better to treat me as your cute little sister...doesn't that sound enticing?

SARAH So, what would you have me do?

LAURA I don't know....I truly don't know!

[THE LIGHTS DIM...SARAH AND LAURA EXIT...THE BENCH IS REMOVED WHEN THE LIGHTS COME UP...ALLYSSIA STANDING NEAR THE BAR OR A FIRE PLACE MANTLE....SHE IS LOOKING AT FAMILY PICTURES....SHE IS HOLDING A DRINK....BEANIE ENTERS]

ALLYSSIA Oh, Beanie....I suppose Beatrice went back to her room....it's not like years ago....she was the provocateur, and still in control.....now, any confrontation sends her back in her room....

BEANIE *[being defensive]* You should know, you're her sister!....

ALLYSSIA I'm sorry Beanie....I was really just making an observation, not a condemnation....you know, we haven't spoke alone for a long time....how are you doing?

BEANIE I believe that I'm all right....you know me....like oil on water, I go with the flow....I just let life take me where it will......

ALLYSSIA Yes....you do....and you're good for Bea....if not for you...I don't know what she'd do.....

BEANIE It's difficult for her....neither of the boys are staying close....she dotes on Michael's letters...but they're few in number...and he rarely says anything important in them....they're more like a child's sleep away camp letters home....and Sam has his own family....he knows the reason Bea put him in Chicago....so he is busy, happy, and pays minimum homage......

ALLYSSIA One hundred percent opposite his lifetime plan......

BEANIE Yes, and now it's even more complicated....she's seriously ill and a lot weaker than she'll admit.....telling Michael some of it....while premeditated...is true..in her mind....this will be the last opportunity to hold Michael close....and to hand him Crane's enterprises on a silver platter....

ALLYSSIA: And if he won't take it?

7 - ONE ACT PLAYS

BEANIE She'll go into a cocoon and die!

ALLYSSIA Beanie...don't say that.....

BEANIE I have to say it....I believe it!

ALLYSSIA How can I help....I don't think she'll confide in me?

BEANIE You can talk to Michael....he always looked up to you... and so did Samuel...help them to understand their mother......she's not the hard bitten woman, she appears to be on the surface....

ALLYSSIA It's not just the surface, but three layers below that too.....

BEANIE There are still more layers to consider....and to find a balance....

ALLYSSIA You've just handed me a monumental task.... monuments are very heavy.....

BEANIE: As you said before....we've known each other a long time....I know to whom I pass the baton...to most, I'm just a figure...a body here.... But in my way, I love your sister....and, I believe she loves me...so I must protect her as best I can.......that's why I'm leaning on you.....

ALLYSSIA Beanie, you've won my heart....I'll start with the surrounding cast...

[BEANIE EXITS...ALLYSSIA LOOKS THE ROOM OVER... SHE TAKES TWO DEEP BREATHS...GOES TO THE BAR...SARAH ENTER]

ALLYSSIA Ah, good.....you're here...have a drink with me...let's sit down and talk...

SARAH I'd like to make it a double....but you'd better keep it neat....pills and liquor aren't close friends....

ALLYSSIA A half jigger it is....how did it go with Laura?

SARAH If a lawyer was there she'd have disowned me on the spot....

ALLYSSIA That bad?

SARAH Boys think their mothers are virgins...girls ..snow white!

ALLYSSIA What will you do?

SARAH To quote Laura...I don't know...I truly don't know....

ALLYSSIA This is not going to be an easy or happy party ..

SARAH That's becoming more and more obvious...

ALLYSSIA Bea has a very special agenda....and I don't think she can pull it off....at least not with two very clear circumstances..... one, that Michael may finally be getting weary of all his world chaos....and two...this is where Laura comes in....that, if he's ready for a comfort zone...he recognizes it in Laura.....

SARAH I told Laura that I didn't know who her father is....

ALLYSSIA Oh dear....what are the odds?

7 - ONE ACT PLAYS

SARAH It was most likely Jacob...Seymour was quite ill at the time....

ALLYSSIA They don't have to have children....

SARAH That hasn't even entered the equation yet...Laura can be disgustingly honest at times...she wouldn't delude Michael... and Bea....for spite...she can infer it also...

[THEY ARE BOTH QUIET FOR A WHILE SIPPING THEIR DRINKS...SUDDENLY ALLYSSIA EXPLODES]

ALLYSSIA The damned truth is that nobody really knows Michael any more....I love him and I don't know him...and I will continue to love him, no matter what....but what the hell is "no matter what?"

[MIICHAEL ENTERS...HE IS SOLID...RUDDY COMPLEXION...DRESSED OUTDOORS CASUAL... CARRIES AN OVERNIGHT SUITCASE...PUTS IT DOWN AND GRABS ALLYSSIA GAYLY]

MICHAEL: *[EMPHATICALLY]*. I'VE BEEN SEARCHING ALL OVER THIS EARTH TO FIND THAT ANSWER.... "What the hell is ...no matter what?"

ALLYSSIA Michael...where did you come from? When did you arrive? And...put me down!

MICHAEL I can't ...I've fallen in love with my beautiful aunt... who looks younger than I do *[AS HE RELEASES HER]*

ALLYSSIA You are so full of blarney....you should have been born Irish...

MICHAEL Would I lie?...Aunt Alyss, you're still ravishing *[NOTING SARAH]* oh, goodness...Sarah...I didn't see you...something in the water here....you're lovely as ever.....

SARAH Thank you Michael...and you're aunt is soft....you're pure bullshit....But more important you look fine...and healthy....and how are you doing?

MICHAEL I'm well...and I'm doing well...where is every body?

ALLYSSIA: Around and about...mother's upstairs...Laura somewhere...and Sam can't get here...no flights from Chicago...he'll come with Evelyn and the kids next weekend....there are others scattered about...you can see them later...right now, you belong to me.....

SARAH I believe I'll tell the others you've arrived... *[SHE EXITS]*

MICHAEL I know Sam's okay....we write to each other all the time....and I call him when the opportunity avails.....but how is my mother...she sounds terrible from her letters...I blew off a major assignment to be here.

ALLYSSIA She hasn't been well for a long time....but you wouldn't know it to be with her....she's a great actress.....you're thirty five now, Michael....and you've been away for a long time....we...she wanted to see you....

MICHAEL It's just that the assignments get more and more critically important....they're hard to walk away from....

ALLYSSIA Michael!...In addition to being your most beautiful aunt, I'm your only one......and I'm your straight shooting aunt.... you're handing me hogwash....you could have been here more often if you wanted to.

MICHAEL You're right Alyss....I could have....and probably should have...but my mother has tunnel vision and I' not comfortable in her tunnel....all she talks about in her letters.... besides telling me how ill she is....is the company....it lacks leadership....it's falling apart....

ALLYSSIA Michael....mother is not well...but she's far from her deathbed.

MICHAEL I know...Sam keeps me updated.....about her...about the company....besides, all the money people I know tell me that Crane's is humming along swimmingly, in fact, they tell me to buy stock.

ALLYSSIA But you Michael....how are you doing? It's been three years since Carolyn was killed....and we hardly know you any more....losing her must have been so difficult...you didn't call on any of us for support....

MICHAEL I couldn't bring it home...it was too personal...and the toughest thing for me was not being with her when it happened... she was too fearless.... I could have protected her better...she was in Africa.... and I stuck in Beirut......

ALLYSSIA That's terrible....I-----

MICHAEL *[GOING ON]* You know, she never took dangerous assignments until she met me....I begged her not to....She hadn't known some of the horrors we live with....nor had she developed the instincts for safety that we have...

ALLYSSIA How could she?....she was never a soldier!

MICHAEL That's right...but God...her sensitivity for people and their agony was incredible.....she taught me to see through her and her camera's eyes....I had always seen death.....but now the vitriolic mindlessness of man...

ALLYSSIA You still haven't told me how you dealt with it.....

MICHAEL My uncle Sam gave me a great education in how to lose friends....or those men who bravely, and without question, followed me into the mouth of the lion....they're still with me....every day....but I also still see the eyes of those who's lives I took....they stare back at me, with puzzled faces.......asking why?....why?...and then the ultimate loss....my wife.....

BEANIE *[ENTERS AND SEES MICHAEL]*.... Michael....Michael...when did you get here? How did you sneak in?

MICHAEL Stealth Beanie....stealth....well you're holding up *[HUGGING]* It's good to see you.....

BEANIE I'm glad you made it for the birthdays....you are so important to her....*[QUIETLY]* why don't we step aside and talk....I need a few moments with you...*[THEY MOVE DOWN RIGHT]* ..Michael, your mother's not at all well.....

MICHAEL So she tells me in her letters....

BEANIE She's even more ill that she'll admit......pancreatic cancer....I doubt she'll last the year

MICHAEL: That, I didn't realize.

BEANIE It's critical that you stay till the end.....

MICHAEL I couldn't do that...stay that long

BEANIE That's a heartless reaction.....her whole life has been devoted to you

MICHAEL You err there my friend....her life has been devoted to herself....Sam and I were puppets....Sam still is...he should kick up his heels and step into the leadership of Crane's......he's more that qualified.....

BEANIE He can't....and that's the point....it's your mother's wish...you are to take that position!

MICHAEL Wrong...I am not a businessman......and never will be...enough of this talk...I need air

BEANIE All right for now....we'll talk again later....I'll tell Beatrice you're here... [HE EXITS

[SARAH AND LAURA BURST INTO THE ROOM.... MICHAEL GRABS LAURA AND TWIRLS HER AROUND]

MICHAEL Ah, here is one of the great loves of my life....

LAURA If you only really meant it....

MICHAEL I mean it…I mean it…you're still so beautiful….how old are you now twelve?

LAURA Bastard!

MICHAEL Okay…okay thirteen!

LAURA Bigger bastard!

MICHAEL I take it all back…except the beautiful part…I won't let that go….

LAURA Now you're being nice….why?

MICHAEL Because I'm here….and you're here…and just about everyone I love is here

LAURA Do you remember the last time you twirled me around like that?

MICHAEL No….not that I recall…

LAURA It was after the final football game at the university…..you had just caught the pass for a touchdown that won the game for us….everyone was celebrating…..

MICHAEL I was lucky….the halfback stumbled and left me alone….you could have caught that pass…..

LAURA But you did and you were the hero….and after the game you grabbed me and twirled me around…and then you kissed me on the lips in front of all those people….you were a senior and I just a soph…I was so proud……

MICHAEL I remember now...you were a great kiss!

LAURA Liar....everybody was so nice to me for weeks...they all wanted to know our relationship... I told them we were secret lovers....that, somehow, made me more important to them

MICHAEL Maybe we should have been?

LAURA At eighteen, that would have been a push for me....

SARAH Laura, I don't believe you would have done that....

LAURA Mother, neither you nor I quite know what I would have done....

MICHAEL Don't I have an opinion here?

LAURA Yes....but no one will pay attention to it!

MICHAEL And Sarah...I haven't forgotten that a good part of my better grades in college and now...being a journalist is because of you....

SARAH Nonsense...I didn't do anything...

MICHAEL You certainly did....how many times did I call you for help with a composition, or a term paper....You taught me to forget the fancy words and to concentrate on story and substance.... you made me more the writer that I am, than any professor that I had.....

SARAH You were an easy student....and a pain in the ass for everything else...always scrounging around for candy.....I remember you pulling Laura's braids when you were eight years old….

MICHAEL It was her fault…she was sweet like candy….and an easy target….I didn't pull them when she was nineteen….

LAURA You should have…I would have loved it….

ALLYSSIA Michael…you've been leading such an exciting life…. you're all over the globe….tell us about it….

MICHAEL It's just like a travelogue Alyss….the best and the worst at the same time….India is a good example….incredibly beautiful landscapes….the delicate, and man designed and built tribute to love that one could imagine…the Taj Mahal in Agra…..and then to see the most abject poverty in so many of the villages…..nothing is as ugly than an extended belly of a child… we, here, in the United States…..it's beyond our comprehension…..

SARAH And it's the latter you've chosen to write about….but we know you have another side….why don't you turn your attention to that, rather than wars and disasters?

MICHAEL I'd like to think that I have another side…and often I think I'd like to turn to it…..I really wish I could………..

SARAH Then what's stopping you?

MICHAEL How can I explain why?….I don't rightly know…. What I do know is that a terribly strong magnet pulls me in one direction….it's like I have to witness all the suffering I see….. and then to open the eyes of mankind to it's own ruthlessly self inflicted shame…..

ALLYSSIA Sounds like a massive project for my little nephew.......

MICHAEL I don't mean to sound narcissistic, or certainly not saintly......I know that what I write, or what I say falls mostly on deaf ears....but I must believe that someone hears me, and does better than he would have done otherwise

LAURA It would be wonderful if you'd write a book Michael... and let me edit it

MICHAEL If I write a book....you're the editor!

LAURA I know everywhere you've been...and somewhat of what you've done....I have a collection of everything you've written, and everything written about you......I've also created a collection of Carolyn's photos and the styles about her work....sometimes I think I know her....even though we couldn't have met.

BEATRICE *[ENTERS ON THE LAST PART OF THE CONVERSATION WITH BEANIE]...* Of course you've never met...Michael neglected to bring her home....

MICHAEL *[RUSHES TO KISS Beatrice]* Hello Mother...I promised for my birthday...finally out of diapers....

BEATRICE You're bit early Michael....birthday is tomorrow.....

MICHAEL I intend to celebrate the whole weekend...you're still the most beautiful woman in the world....It's no wonder Beanie doesn't let you alone...he's keeping away all those gentlemen callers.....

MICHAEL *[WITHOUT ANGER]* there are many places one can call home, mother.....

BEATRICE *[VERY EMOTIONAL]* Home is where you were born...and where you grew up. *[GETTING EVEN MORE EXCITED]* and where you were schooled....and where you were-----

ALYSSIA *[INTERRUPTING]* Bea,! Slow down I don't let yourself get so excited!!

BEATRICE *[SLOWLY AND DELIBERATELY NOW]* and where you were nurtured.....

ALYSSIA *[BREAKING THE TENSION]* And now you're a movie star too?

MICHAEL Oh sure,...a movie star.....a walk on role playing a foreign journalist....for most of the scene all I did was stand to the side and look serious...

LAURA Between two semi-nude twenty year-olds with sculpted bodies and faces like Aphrodite...

MICHAEL I didn't say the work was hard...

BEANIE Get me into the next film, Michael, I'll gladly play your father in that setting

SARAH I'm sure you would....you men can be so shallow.....

BEANIE Even in water up to your knees...better than no water at all

7 - ONE ACT PLAYS

BEATRICE That's enough banter.... Now, if you will all indulge me, I'd like a few words with Michael alone

ALYSSIA As you wish, big sister.....

[THEY ALL EXIT. Beatrice remains seated....Michael stands just upstage of her]

BEATRICE Michael, you know what I'm going to say....

MICHAEL Yes....and I don't want you to say it....

BEATRICE You must hear me out.....I certainly deserve that much....

MICHAEL [***SETTLING INTO A CHAIR***] Yes...you do...I'll listen and try not to say anything.......

BEATRICE You do not really remember your father very well.... he was a good man....but ineffectual.....he inherited Crane's from his father and grandfather...but controlling it was over his head.... so he abdicated control and handed it over to others.....

MICHAEL They've done a helluva job with it....it's quite prosperous....

BEATRICE Not in small measure to the fact that I've been the CEO all these years....I have the head for this business that your father didn't have......

MICHAEL What's your point?

BEATRICE My point, as you put it, is simple......I have sat in the key seat and carried the weight long enough....I must stop... it's time for you to take it....

MICHAEL But, I don't want it!

BEATRICE Michael, you cannot live your life as you have these last year's indefinitely ....it has to end....you have a responsibility....you are to assume the role you were born to......

MICHAEL Mother, do you hear yourself?...you are not the Queen Mother...and I am not the Prince of Wales......

BEATRICE You were bred for this role....you have the leadership skills that your father lacked...even the soldiers who served under you, in Vietnam, have told me so....the army doesn't give medals away without a reason....

MICHAEL Leading soldiers and leading business heads are two very different things.....mother, my degrees are in philosophy and psychology....you already have the perfect man to lead Crane's..... your son....my brother Sam....he's certainly qualified.....and you know that.....

BEATRICE *[PLEADING NOW]* But you are the older brother.... and you have demonstrated the skills.....

MICHAEL Only in your mind....don't you realize how Sam has grown the Chicago office? ..hand the reins to me mother and I will pass them right to Sam....

BEATRICE *[very upset]* Michael...I will not!!

MICHAEL MOTHER....STOP IT....*[CALMING DOWN]* now, calm down...we've talked enough for now.....there are guests...let's not spoil the birthday party....*[EXITS] [BEATRICE IS LEFT ALONE ON STAGE FOR FEW MOMENTS...SHE IS OBVIOUSLY TORN ...ALYSSIA ENTERS AND SEES HER]*

ALYSSIA Are you all right Bea?

BEATRICE He won't listen to me Alyss.....

ALYSSIA Of course he won't....he's not that boy....or that man.... that you any longer would like him to be.....

BEATRICE He can't be allowed to go back to those jungles or..... whatever place they send him....he'll be hurt....or worse.....and I need him here....to be near me....to run Crane's

ALYSSIA Which is it Bea? .....for him?....for Crane's....or for you?

BEATRICE That's not fair!

ALYSSIA Fair?....maybe not? but, it is accurate....

BEATRICE I don't care.....I won't give in...... I want my son back.....

ALLYSSIA You have another son...do you want him back too?

BEATRICE It isn't the same.....he never left....he is here....!

ALLYSSIA He's not here ...he's in Chicago...where you exiled him....how often do you see him?....or Evelyn? Or the children?....

how well do you know them...or they, you? How often do they visit?.....

ALYSSIA They're not close.....they're almost as far away as Michael!

BEATRICE That's not true.....my sons are the men in my life.... it's through them that I replace my husband........

ALYSSIA *[GETTING VERY ANGRY WITH HER]* Beatrice... when, in God's name are going to stop being delusional?.....you will lose your sons completely if you keep this nonsense up....don't you realize what you're doing.....how you keep them, and everyone else, at arm's length?....and you've been doing it for so long that its' become an ugly pattern .....and you are the face of that pattern,.... you can't dictate....it's repellant.... You sent those you love away because they can't understand you....and so they're afraid to touch you....rather than fight you, they stay at a distance...away from your tongue.....and, I suppose Beanie, what have you done to him? Hypnosis?

BEATRICE Beanie's not the issue....Michael is!!

ALYSSIA Bea....for Christ's sake.....stop.....take the time to listen....time to understand....and when you do, you will see Michael and Sam as they are...not what your imagination prefers to see!!.....

BEATRICE But Michael has a duty...!...

ALYSSIA Damn it....Michael has a duty....but to himself first... he's not the boy you sent to war....that boy is gone....you must appreciate the man he's become....

BEATRICE *[BROKEN AND IN TEARS]*....I try!....I try! It is so difficult for me...he tries to explain so much to me....I hear him talking....but I can't listen....I lose his meaning.....my mind wanders to other times....I see him in school or in a convertible...I try so hard....it doesn't work....Alyss...maybe if you speak to him... you would make better sense of those things he says than I.....and then you can make them clear to me.....

ALYSSIA Yes...I will....but only if you promise that you'll be the person you are at this moment.....

[BEATRICE USES HER HEAD MOTIONS AND SOFT NESS TO AGREE AS MICHAEL COMES IN ON A HIGH NOTE]

MICHAEL Mother, I was just with Alex Sutherland....what a wonderful mind that man has....he's planning to take Crane's into Asia....starting with Vietnam....and hopefully, in the near future, China....he wanted my sense of the people and the societies there....my God,....he and I could talk for hours.....

BEATRICE That's wonderful Michael.....you should work with him....I rely on him for almost everything.....but now, I must check on the kitchen staff....make sure they don't run out of those little hot dogs that everyone seems to like so much....*[EXITS]*

MICHAEL *[EFFUSIVELY]* ....Alissia Godwin...my dear sweet aunt....I wasn't joking before when I said you are still beautiful..... and vibrant....and...why haven't you remarried?

ALYSSIA To you I may be beautiful and vibrant...not necessarily to others....so, if you want to marry this old lady?....I'm all yours, my sweet nephew.

MICHAEL I'm a journalist....I'm very objective....I see beauty and life....when it's there.

ALYSSIA Thank you dear....but Michael...at the moment, it's you that we worry about...you seem so lost...how do we reach out to you?

MICHAEL Arms can't reach that far....they're intersected by too many breaks....but the thought that somebody might want to reach out to me is the comforting solicitude that maintains my sanity......ALLYSS, I've been trying to understand myself.....and my mother....*[HE HESITATES]* Alysss, what was my father really like? I only remember him in a fog.....

ALYSSIA He was a beautiful man...tall and rangy....very smart....a philosopher in many ways.....and quite impractical.....he ran Crane's.....but he had a disease that would take him young....and he knew it...that's why he established a leadership in Crane's that would run without him....I suppose that he expected that you or Sam..or both of you, would eventually take over....

MICHAEL But, ..he and my mother?

ALYSSIA Oh, she was beautiful and smart also....and driven....and your father was rich.....

MICHAEL It always seemed illusional, or a bad marriage....he was rarely home...

ALYSSIA Your mother was quite insistant on many things....things she wanted....or wanted to do....your father was not confrontational....to avoid battles, he'd go elsewhere....it goes back a ways....we were all friends in college....Bea, Sarah, and Myself...

hers was an unfortunate marriage in one sense and your father's in another...Sarah and your father became lovers....he could not and would not fight with your mother...she had her own lovers....

MICHAEL Beanie?

ALYSSIA Among others....he was one of the tennis pros at the country club....quite a dashing young man at the time....then and now....he's been very handy to have around

MICHAEL I remember your husband, my uncle Max....he was a happy outgoing man...always found time to be at my baseball and football games...even wore the university sweater...in some ways, my substitute father.....

ALLYSSIA And I remember the young man who left home too many years ago....where is he? Why doesn't he come home?

MICHAEL I can no longer be that person...I can't fit into that body again.....I'd contaminate it with my actions, my experiences.... someone once said "We do not pass through the same door twice, nor return through the door we passed."

ALLYSSIA Many men leave home and go to war....ot whatever else....and they return to family...and have a family....

MICHAEL Don't you think that I longed to return to a life with even a semblance of normality....picnics and football games.... they can't exist for me again....one can't jump from a placid life to one of horror....and then return again...not if you have any sense of empathy in your psyche....for what you've seen ot what you've done? there is no easy escape...I've tried.....

ALLYSSIA Michael, you are so hard to understand……

MICHAEL How can I explain?….If you take a life…or many lives….you must try to give back….it's an impossible task….but one that must be pursued….if not, your demons will follow you….haunt and devour you…until that time your eyes close…..

ALLYSSIA Michael, you make me love you more….even if I can't know what's inside your head….you will do what you must do…and I will support you in it….but go easy on your mother…she's both mentally and physically frail…..despite her exterior and superior attitudes….and..remember….she loves you too…

[LIGHTS DIM FOR A PASSAGE OF TIME…BOTH EXIT]

[MICHAEL ENTERS WITH LAURA AND THEY ARE BOTH LAUGHING]

MICHAEL That'd supposed to be a sedate crowd out there….I don't know if we can afford the liquor bill?

LAURA It's always the quiet ones that get you….you know that….

MICHAEL By the way, your mother's been almost silent…..

LAURA Ever since the outburst of who my father may be….I think she's in shock over the admission….not the revelation….I never heard her say it before…you know, I never knew either of them….my father by name, or yours….they both died so early…..

MICHAEL At least I had my uncle Max….he was pretty good guy….

LAURA Allyssia says you're like your father in many ways....a philosopher who runs away...you to war, he to my mother.....

MICHAEL He did better than me....but it's a kind of simplistic analysis, don't you think?

LAURA I don't know what to think....we've been kind of fencing with each other the last half hour...Michael,...are we brother and sister?

MICHAEL It's a happy thought...for me anyway....I wish I could say yes with certainty....but I'm glad to yes even to the possibility....

LAURA Part of me wants to say yes, and the other part doesn't... because the other part wants you to fall in love with me....and to take me to where ever you go...and to share in whatever you're doing....

MICHAEL But Laura we may be-----

LAURA That doesn't matter, just as long as we're together....we need not have children.....

MICHAEL Children are not the issue...I won't bring more children into this world there are too many already that need help

LAURA All the more reason...we can be a team..we can do so much good.....

MICHAEL How could I take you with me?....The last woman who joined me paid for the privilege with her life....and she isn't the only woman I worked with who succumbed to wounds... mental and physical....

LAURA I would understand.....

MICHAEL How could you?...someone who has never been there....how would you relate?...relate to the smells....the heat...searing flesh....the ever constant death....all become an anesthetic, an out of body experience...hovering over a never ending holocaust....a degradation of the human experience.

LAURA All the more-----

MICHAEL [CONTINUING] It's like a virus, eating away at your flesh.....and this is only part of the scene.....you could never understand, nor would I want you to

LAURA [TRYING TO BE FORCEFUL] Michael!!! ... you are not the first man to go into hell....others have gone before you...both men and women...I'm not the child you once knew...I'm a strong woman....

MICHAEL Laura, it's not you....to believe you're my sister makes me love you more...but with the added need to protect you....

LAURA And I would protect you.....

MICHAEL But not from my demons....since the first time...in the jungle....men, women, children,....just walking into the guns...and the guns kept firing....but they still kept walking...eyes staring at me...and they still stare...wherever I go....and now they're joined by others....from wherever I've been....China...deep Africa....they follow me into the finest hotels of this earth....into my sleep, at dinner, they won't leave me

LAURA Michael, ..I.._____

7 - ONE ACT PLAYS

MICHAEL [CONTINUING] And they won't leave until all the viciousness and killing and hunger on this earth disappear..... and we know that it's an unending quest

LAURA And must you follow this quest alone?....even Quiote had Sancho Panza....I could be both Sancho and Dulcinea......

MICHAEL [SOFTENED TO HER ALLUSIONS} Can I let those ghosts destroy all who come near me....no......I can't...... there may be only one way to end them....and that's to end me.... why it hasn't happened yet?.....I don't know.....maybe they're just teasing me?

[LAURA CAN'T TAKE IT ANY MORE....SHE RUNS FROM THE ROOM CRYING MISCHAEL GOES TO THE BAR TAKES A STIFF DRINK.....STARES AT IT FOR A MOMENT....THEN GULPS IT DOWN....BEATRICE ENTERS]

BEATRICE Why did Laura run out of this room crying?.....what did you say to her?

MICHAEL WE talked....we're friends.....brother and sister even....but a situation that neither of us can be happy with......

BEATRICE I hope you weren't cruel.....

MICHAEL I hope so too.....I tried not to be.....

BEATRICE Michael,....I asked Allyssia to talk to you

MICHAEL I know....we talked.....

BEATRICE She said that you won't take Crane's ....that you will continue your odyssey

MICHAEL It may not make sense to you....but I have no choice... It doesn't mean I love you less...or Sam and the children....It's just that I've fallen out of the society here

BEATRICE: What's wrong with the society here?

MICHAEL Nothing...at least not in the context of our discussion .....but there exists a much larger society, and there's a lot wrong with it....it has a trillion wounds....and perhaps....only perhaps....I can put a band aid on a few.....

BEATRICE What you do is dangerous!

MICHAEL Not nearly as dangerous as what many others do....

BEATRICE Your wife....who I never met, was killed and she was not supposed to do the things you pursue.....

MICHAEL I know that...and that guilt plagues me......

BEATICE Then there's nothing that------

MICHAEL *[INTERRUPTING]* Nothing...I will leave again in a few weeks.....I want to spend time with you and Allyss.....and with Sam and the kids when they get here next week.....

BEATRICE What about Laura?

MICHAEL I know the full story....and I'm going to explain it to Sam.....she's a lovely woman....one easy to love...and I'm going to love her....as a sister, but no more....I doubt that any woman will fit into my future.....and you should love Laura too....make amends with Sarah.....you need her friendship more that you think....

BEATRICE You've only been here a few hours and already you're tidying up family affairs.....you could apply the talent to Crane's....

MICHAEL Sam will do a better job......

BEATRICE I still can't know what happened to you that has made you this way

MICHAEL Let's just say that I was wounded in a war of phantoms....and what happened is just as important as what did not happen.....wars don't end.....they go on.....they relocate....a chess game run by the Gods....and I have become a pawn.....and, I suppose, a willing pawn......

BEATRICE And yet, my child

MICHAEL And happy to be your child.....especially on a birthday day like today......do you realize....they haven't brought out the cake yet *[SHOUTING]* hey Beanie....where's the cake?.....I want to sing happy birthday.......

[LIGHT DOWN SLOW....FINAL CURTAIN]

IN PURSUIT OF

A ONE ACT PLAY

BY JERRY 'JOSH' KONSKER

CAST OF CHARACTERS:
ALAN KANTREL: 35yo ASSOCIATE PROFESSOR OF ENGLISH LITERATURE
GUY PEARSON: 45yo ASSOCIATE PROFESSOR OF POLITICAL SCIENCE
HAMILTON PHOEBUS: 60yo PROFESSOR AND CHAIRMAN OF THE ENGLISH DEPT.
JANET SMYTHE: 32yo FRIEND OF ALAN
ABBY: 40yo ALAN'S OLDER SISTER
JOHN: 42yo ABBY'S HUSBAND
FRED: 40yo FAMILY FRIEND
CATHY: 39yo FRED'S WIFE

STUDENTS:.......JAMES WHISTLER.....MARY ELLEN BROWN....ETHAN JANOWITZ...

ESTELLE VELEZ.....SARAH SCHOEN.....HERMAN LEE WANG

SETTING: *[A SEMINAR CLASSROOM IN A SMALL MIDWESTERN UNIVERSITY NINE CHAIRS AND A HEAD TABLE....GUY AT THE TABLE....ALL OTHERS*

SEATED IN A SEMICIRCLE FACING THE TABLE........ ALAN ENTERS LEFT]

GUY: [LIGHTLY] It's about time you showed up.......using the stairs again instead of the elevator?

ALAN: Stairs always...otherwise I'll get pudgy like you........

GUY: [TO THE STUDENTS] Do you hear how he talks to his superiors?,...no respect......and this is the man you made me invite here today....

ALAN: I bow to you, oh oracle of the English department.!

GUY: Alan....or shall I call you professor Kantrel......to the business at hand.... other than Professor Phoebus, who is your direct boss.....are the leading members of the student government and the political science club at the college.....

ALAN: Assistant Professor please...I am still a humble man.....

GUY: Anyway, Alan, there is a method to our madness.....you know....I believe.....all of the students here today......

ALAN: Yup!.....they've all been unfortunate or silly enough to take one or more of my classes.....

JAMES: [JUMPING IN] That's it professor.....your classes on politics in literature....the effect of social consciousness on governments by writers......the same as the McClure group with Teddy Roosevelt.

GUY: Alan, the group....and many others on campus...........they've been studying conditions in our national government' scene.....

MARY ELLEN: [INTERJECTING} We've come to the conclusion that both stink....we have a congress in lockjaw....

ALAN: That's a rather succinct description Mary....I don't disagree with you, but how do I fit in?

ETHAN: [BEING A BIT DEVIOUS]....You see professor,.... professors Phoebus and Pearson have joined with us to form a political action committee......we want to do something to effect this present condition....we thought you'd like to join us....

ALAN: Sounds like a noble ambition....count me in....but this looks like more than a simple recruiting meeting.....Guy Pearson could have gotten me to join over a morning cup of coffee.....

[THE STUDENTS GET MORE AND MORE INTENSE AS THEY CONTINUE]

ESTELLE: [SHEEPISHLY...SHE ACTS AS IF SHE HAS A STUDENT CRUSH ON ALAN] Well, what we thought should be addressed is congressman Blakely....he usually is on a fence waiting to see which way the wind is blowing....he's lazy and ineffective

HERMAN: [INTERRUPTING] He's over the hill...he's an old man........

ALAN: Again, I don't really disagree.....and being old isn't a sin.....also, ousting a sitting legislator is a tall order......We're a school of forty five hundred in a city of, maybe one hundred seventy five thousand....and in our congressional district of a little more than four hundred thousand.....and it's spread out..... how do you expect----------

SARAH: [STANDING AND VERY CONTROLLED] Professor.....we may be novices....but we're not totally naïve..... we've done our homework....there is one college, two community colleges and one tech college, besides us in the district. And then to the high schools.....we would get kids active with and them to their ambivalent parents... basic level....about five hundred thousand should do it......that's little more than a dollar a voter... We're not going to spend on TV advertising Obama raised zillions on the internet.....we're pretty good at that too...it should be enough....

HERMAN: My uncle offered us an empty store front on Main Street in town, it's the perfect campaign headquarters......

MARY ELLEN: The summer's coming...we'll all stay on campus and we already have over two hundred recruits with more joining everyday.....we're now adding more at the other schools....so, with four months of work until the September primaries, we have eight weeks to get the first part of the job done..

SARAH: We know it's a lot of intense campaigning......but soon we'll be thousands strong......door to door....in public places..... and even in rural areas.....

ALAN: Guy....Hamilton.... God bless ambitious youth. Compile an alphabetical list of all volunteers. Their addresses, phones, age, etc. How long have you been working on this? Be able to add to the list weekly.

ETHAN: Almost two months now.....

ALAN: I don't want to be a spoiler......but have you thought of the down side of this? Winning an election of this type is a long shot.....and you're asking for a lot of work....more probably, than most of you have ever put forth.....even in one of my classes.

JAMES: There is no down side.....just the experience is an education.....for us graduating seniors......that may be all we'll get.....But for the under classmen, maybe Professor Pearson might consider it worth three credits or more.....but, if I may, ...we're not in it just for the experience, or for the game, or for credits..... we truly believe that a change in the congressman is needed..... for both the district and the country..... a lot of people have given much more of themselves and accomplished much less.......

ALAN: All right....what would you have me do as part of this undertaking? I can quote Coleridge and I've written jingles for pretzels......

ESTELLE: Our search committee....oh yes, we have one....came up with a description of the person who should be our candidate...... young....very smart...well spoken and charismatic....a magnetic personality.....and with a clear understanding, supplemented by an open mind, of our government and it's responsibilities..... [POINTING AT ALAN AS DO ALL THE STUDENTS AND FACULT... THEY ALL APPLAUD. THEN SIT AS ALAN SPEAKS]

ALAN: Whoa....hold on a second......Guy....I thought you were my friend....I thought the students liked me.....Why me?

GUY: Alan, don't be modest.....you fit the description to a tee.... the kids really believe in you.....and with your record as a war hero....you're a natural.....

ALAN: Hey....wait a minute ...I'm no hero,....I--------

GUY: Bullshit.....they don't give out silver stars for marksmanship.....Alan, as James said this is our country.....what was it in those World War II posters [UNCLE SAM WANTS YOU]......Alan, you underestimate yourself.....Uncle Sam needs you....and you are looking at a very dedicated group of young Americans who want you to be their leader.....every member of the faculty I've spoken to fully concurs and pledges to assist and take part in all our endeavors.......

ALAN: Wow....I'm overwhelmed....I'm flattered...I do agree with you guys....our district's repped by a tired old man......and he is reelected every two years by a tired apathetic community.....but me as his replacement? That's a stretch......I don't know if I'm up to it.....there's a lot of things you guys don't know about......you're not aware that I have a serious intestinal problem. Since they never were able to get all the shrapnel out of my stomach....I don't know if I'm physically up to such a task.....mentally?....I would hope so....but there could be a problem....

JAMES: Fair enough professor.....please think about it....take your time....we really want you....trust you....but with or without you we're going forward...and we're ready to assist you acting as your aides....the girls all love you.....

ALAN: Okay for the moment....but the teacher in me requires something more of you than what you've already offered.....I give you my promise that I will seriously consider what you ask....there are obstacles that I must overcome....I must and will talk to my doctors....so everything stays open....at least at this time....but I also want from you and at least two dozen others.... A 1500 word explanation and commitment of self examination......remember, if I run....I'm a centrist....are you comfortable with that?......or include anything you wish...but no platitudes....I'll ask professors Phoebus and Pearson to review them with me....You have four days to prepare them leaving us three to look them over....we will meet again at this time next week......you can expand the committee as you like....[ALAN PAUSES] ...This could prove to be one of the most important decisions you make in your lifetime....it most certainly would be in mine......[AS THE STUDENTS BREAK UP ALAN CONTINUES]. Guy....Hamilton......would you stay a few moments? I'd like to speak to you....[THE STUDENTS LEAVE AND THE THREE MEN SIT AT THE TABLE] .... Are you two out of your minds? Have these kids any idea of what they have undertaken? ...the magnitude......and Guy....what's worse....you're their leader!

GUY: Only until you take over.....you're a natural leader did you hear yourself these last few minutes....you've already taken over.... you're their leader....now, I'm your assistant.....

ALAN: Why don't you run....your much more knowledgeable than all of us.....

GUY: Alan....look at me ......I'm a middle aged short fat guy with glasses....I was a class nerd....no....the wrong image....we don't need an ugly duckling....we need a swan.....

ALAN: I hope that was a bad joke....

GUY: Not really....you have a long neck.....but seriously Alan.... you know that the students and others attach themselves to you.... and you know that the world attaches itself and admires pretty people....you're no Adonis Alan....but you're a tall, strong and solid image......add that to your other qualities, and we have a very viable, electable candidate.....

HAMILTON: Let me interrupt....I'm the old man here....but when James and the student council came to us with the idea....Alan, I don't remember anything seeming so right.....They'd been discussing it for months.....no dissenting voices....They have hundreds more lined up already....and not all students.....and it's always been you they want.....Alan, in my thirty years of teaching, I've never been able to mesmerize and motivate students like you do...Let's widen their horizons....It's supposed to be what we're all about......

GUY: Alan....these kids will work their tails off for you...and for no pay....they believe in their country and they believe in you....

ALAN: But I've never shown them that I wanted more than I'm doing.....

HAMILTON: Of course you have....you're the one who created courses on politics in literature....you're the one who filled their heads with Dumas, Coleridge, and Whitman....with Shakespeare, and Arthur Miller, ...Spinoza, Odets....Shall I go on?

ALAN: Okay, okay....so I created a monster......however I----------

HAMILTON: You can expand their universe as well as your own.....you're too good to remain here....as much as I value you....Alan! leading, legislating, arguing for the right things, is teaching also....and better....because it's by example....and to a much larger audience.....

ALAN: So, you want me to be the lead monster?

7 - ONE ACT PLAYS

GUY: Before your head swells, my dear friend.....and before we get redundant....let me sum up....I won't count your money, Alan, but I understand that you have a considerable largesse...and that it keeps on coming.....you don't need any major contributors for support you're free of lobbyists.....your military record will move you right to the head of the class.....if we created, from scratch, the perfect candidate....you would fit the mold.....

ALAN: I appreciate your thoughts...truly....but this is too much to digest quickly....I gave the kids four days to delve into their own thinking....we must do that also.....

GUY: By the way....if you married that girlfriend of yours, it wouldn't hurt the campaign....voters like a family man.....

[DIM LIGHTS ...END OF SCENE ONE]

[STAY DIM FOR A SHORT WHILE RESETTING FOR SCENE TWO .....A STARBUCKS TYPE COFFE SHOP ....A TABLE AND THREE CHAIRS DOWN CENTER...A COFFEE BAR UPSTAGE.....ALAN IS SEATED AT THE TABLE READING A NEWSPAPER......A LARGE PAPER CUP OF COFFEE ON THE TABLE.....JANET RUSHES IN FROM UPSTAGE....SHE THROWS HER PURSE ON AN EMPTY CHAIR AND SITS QUICKLY.... SHE IS AN ATTRACTIVE WOMAN THIRTY YEARS OLD.....WEARING MAN TAILORED CLOTHING.... ALAN PUTS HIS PAPER DOWN AS SHE KISSES HIM ON THE CHEEK]

JANET: Waiting long?

ALAN: About three months....anything new in your life today?

JANET: The usual for an assistant DA.....we put away a Dillinger would be.....the son of Sam....and about forty assorted criminals.....

ALAN: I guess it was quiet.....

JANET: Not really....busy, but not crazy.....and your life?

ALAN: Crazy......and confusing....and very serious....

JANET: First, let me get some coffee....and then you can tell me all about it.....do you need refill? [ALAN SHAKES HIS HEAD NO....JAN GETS UP AND GOES UPSTAGE...ALAN PUTS THE PAPERAWAY AND TAKES A WRITING PAD FROM HIS BRIEFCASE AND PUTS IT ON THE TABLE... JAN RETURNS WITH THE COFFEE]

JANET: A pad and pen? This is serious....you're not pregnant, I hope?

ALAN: Worse than that....with pregnancy, you have a fair idea of the outcome.....[HE TAKES A DEEP BREATH]. I was cornered today by Guy Pearson and a chunk of the student body.....they've put together a political action group....they want congressman Blakely replaced in the 512th.....

JANET: That's not a bad idea....he's not particularly effective.....

ALAN: Yes.....and they've chosen someone to run against him....to be the guinea pig.....

JANET: Who'd they find?

ALAN: You're not getting the picture....it's me....they want me to run....you had to be there....it was surreal....the whole meeting....I participated....but when it was over, I had to ask myself what happened.....

JANET: Wow.....what did you tell them?

ALAN: I told them whoa....that I'm flattered...flabbergasted and a few other things...but that we all needed to think it over carefully.....and then Guy suggested that we get married.....

JANET: That's a wonderful idea....I'll make him my maid of honor.....

ALAN: Careful....Guy could accept that role......

JANET: What's to think about? You'd be a great candidate....and a better congressman....even I'd vote for you...and my mother.....I can't swear for my father.....

ALAN: There's a lot to think about....am I qualified?

JANET: Of course you are!!

ALAN: And then, do the kids fully realize what such a campaign requires?....time, money, ...devotion....is congressman Blakely that vulnerable? Do I have the stamina?.....my digestion will always be lousy and the doctors are still watching the shrapnel they haven't been able to get to.....even after all these years...

JANET: Alan, you've started to play racquetball again and some golf....you would be fine.....

ALAN: Then we would have to set a date and I buy you a ring......

JANET: I'm all for that.....just go with me....I'll buy my own ring and call it a campaign expense.....

ALAN: Baby,..I can't do that to you......

JANET: [VERY STRONG] Alan! We've discussed this a million times....when we're ready for children, we'll adopt!!

ALAN: [EQUALLY STRONG] Children are not the issue.....you're too young to repress your libido......and too young to marry a eunuch!!

JANET: [STILL STRONG...MATCHING HIM] Screw my libido....I'm a twenty eight year old woman......I've had enough libido....I don't ever want to hear the word eunuch again.....I've never been close to the sense of love that I feel for you and from you....we have and we will find other ways......

ALAN: [very upset] Damn it to hell....I'm not a whole man....the shrapnel took care of that...you're entitled to a whole man.....

JANET: Stop feeling sorry for yourself....and for me....I'll decide what I'm entitled to...now, quiet down and let's discuss this like two intelligent adults.....

ALAN: Right now, I don't feel so intelligent.....or adult

JANET: Okay....one adult and one dummy....Alan....I love you....this is not "The Sun Also Rises."....and I'm not Brett Ashley who's going to jump into bed with half the men she meets.

ALAN: You needn't make that much of a sacrifice.....you must.....

JANET: Oh, shut up already.....I'm talking now......the question is...are you qualified for congress "that's a no brainer....analyze it....you are young....and you're quite healthy, despite the war wounds.....

ALAN: What do you mean despite the ------

JANET: I said quiet....the service....the wounds.....the silver staar.... And that you're handsome....all that will help you...it certainly worked for John Kennedy....your knowledge of history and politics through literature, puts you miles ahead of anyone else....especially Blakely....your thinking is global...Blakely is homespun....a good old boy.....

ALAN: People like a good old boy......

JANET: Hush!....people, especially young people, cling to you like fly paper, ...your classes are always over requested.... you'd have that same effect on all adults and seniors....I remember my grandfather....you think just like he did...called himself a Rockefeller Republican.....socially liberal and fiscally conservative...middle of the road...you fit that to a tee....

ALAN: Do I have the right to ask so much of others...for me to go to the head of the class?

JANET: Alan....they want you at the head of the class....you've a brilliant mind...you're both soft spoken and out spoken.... And you're the most caring man I've ever met....You even like hamsters....I'll stop there.....Alan...you would be an incredibly marvelous congressman....

ALAN: [HALF LAUGHING] let's see now.....you, your mother, my sister and her husband...me....that's five votes....the rest will be hard work.....

JANET: You're meeting with guy and the committee in less than a week....you gave them homework to restudy their opinions and their commitment.....you do yours....I'll help you....I'm your biggest fan.....

[DIM LIGHTS....END OF SCENE TWO....OPENING SCENE THREE....A LIVING ROOM OF JOHN AND ABBY....COMFORTABLE, BUT NOT OPULENT.... FOUR SOFT CAHIRS....COFFEE TABLE... TWO SMALL TABLES WITH LAMPS ON THEM...ALAN IS SEATED CENTER LEFT.....JOHN IS ON HIS FEET TALKING... MIDDLE THIRTIES...GETTING A BIT PAUNCHY....]

JOHN: What's to think about?........go for it.....

ALAN: And Jan wants to get married....I think------

JOHN: Another think?........ That girl's a pure gem....a sure winner....go for that too....

ALAN: I'd have to give up my position at the college to run....there's no guarantee that it'll still be there if I lose.....

JOHN: You can always come back to my advertising agency....you were a money machine....I'd love to have you full time......in the few lousy months you worked for me, you managed to write a jingle for Peter Piper's Perfect Pretzels....you made us both a small fortune.....and now you're teaching..for something short of a hundred thousand a year....for me, it's a win win...a brother in-law that I can brag about or a copy writer that's a cash cow.....

ALAN: You know, the press will search my history carefully.. my scholastic records are kind of ordinary....and no PHD from Harvard or Yale.....

JOHN: And when they search your military record....they'll come up with a lot of top grades...they don't give out medals for cleaning barracks......Man, you Saved an entire platoon, almost by yourself.....

ALAN: By accident....I was pinned down....couldn't move...

JOHN: That's crap......you exposed yourself....drew fire....so your platoon could slip away and flank the gun emplacement....and then they came back for you

ALAN: I didn't have much choice....

JOHN: The choice was to order someone else to do it......

ALAN: That wasn't a choice....these were my men....

JOHN: That's what I mean......you're a natural leader....you can be great as a congressman or anything else you choose to do.....do you realize I'm your brother in law?...and I still think that you're a terrific person....now, how many brother's in law do you know that can say that?

ABBY: [ENTERS...SHE IS A GOOD LOOKING WOMAN...A FEW YEARS OLDER THAN ALAN] You two are still gabbing?...which company do you wish to destroy with some of your less that brilliant ideas.?

ALAN: John was just telling me how much he loves me.....

ABBY: I glad he does, because I'm not sure that I still do.....I have one brother and he has a death wish....

ALAN: Ab,...you're exaggerating.....

ABBY: [VERY SERIOUS]...Like hell I am......I'm not even concerned with your shrapnel wounds....they'll heal in time..... but that damn shell took half your stomach too....that's what's screwed up....your diet.... you have to eat on time....only special foods....special cooking....

ALAN: I've had that problem for the last eight years...I've done okay.....

ABBY: Sure, here in Lake City, where I can keep an eye on my only little brother.....and feed him twice a week....who's going to take care of you in Washington?

ALAN: I can afford to hire a cook....

JOHN: If he's smart, he'll also have Janet....

ABBY: [GOING ON] and what will the impact be of all the travel and stress...not to mention the demands of your time that everybody will want?

ALAN: Sis, slow down a bit....I only said that I was considering to run...but if I were, I wouldn't be the only or first man to run and to serve in office with war wounds......Bob Dole was a senator and ran for president with his left side practically useless....you know what McCain went through... and the senator from Hawaii with one arm....there were and are many others....I'm still in my thirties...

ABBY: I only want the best for you Alan....In my opinion, you could run this country....let alone this district...I trust you implicitly....you would never do anything callously or deceitfully.... or anything for your own gain...but don't let your ambition blur your brain.

ALAN: But sis,----

ABBY: Don't sis me!......our mother is no longer with us to tell you the truth....so I will have to....[SHE GETS VERY SERIOUS... AND STANDS ABOVE ALAN...OR ON THE ARM OF THE CHAIR}.....Alan, nobody knows better than I do, how important your service to and your love of this country has always driven you....but you've already served this country, and given more of yourself than anyone should ever have to.....

ALAN: Yes, but-------

ABBY: Just listen to me....you love what you're doing....the teaching....the mixing with young people and growing minds..... you're very good at it....everyone tells me so.....don't give that up!!

ALAN: I love you sis....and I know that you love me....you're right....I am in love with my job.....but, what's being asked of me is so important...and so fulfilling...and, honestly, so very tempting.....I have to give it real thought...and I'm meeting again with the committee tomorrow.....

ABBY: I know your head….and whatever you do, I'll be with you…..but you must be careful…..now let's eat….I've ground up some mush for you!!….. [DIM LIGHTS END OF SCENE THREE…..OPEN SCENE FOUR….THE SAME SETS AS SCENE ONE…..GUY, HAMILTON, AND ALAN ARE ON STAGE….HAMILTON IS SEATED AT THE TABLE OTHERS ON THEIR FEET]

GUY: Well, what did you think of their homework assignment?

ALAN: I was surprised at the depth of their understanding…… no super ficialities….and a real desire to move this nation…..and to move it with integrity

HAMILTON: Their papers are a bravo performance…..pleasantly individual and still singular of purpose…..

ALAN: I'm glad I didn't have to grade them for grammar…..at least they have spell check….some of the passages are streams of consciousness….

GUY: Nevertheless, these people are for real….they've learned and grown to be caring adults in their years here…..I'm almost flattered to think that I had something to do with it…..but one thing is obvious….we must consider them quite seriously…..

HAMILTON: I certainly agree….I can hear them coming in now…..

[THE STUDENTS ENTER….MILD GREETINGS….. ALAN STAYS ON HIS FEET TO START THE MEETING.]

7 - ONE ACT PLAYS

ALAN: I must tell everyone....you absolutely floored us....we knew you cared.....we knew you had a good understanding of our government....but your understanding of it's people....their strengths....their weaknesses and fears....as well as your own..... Guy, Ham and I agree....your are more deserving of even more respect than we could have imagined......

HERMAN: [JOKING] Hell, we could have told you that professor......

ALAN: Yes you could....I probably wouldn't have believed you..... but let's put humor aside for the moment......let's analyze what you've given us and given to yourselves.....and remember, this is no longer "a you and we" effort....this is us......

MARY ELLEN: Are you flattering us? I think we're above that......

ALAN: You are..... this is simply the next logical step.....it's a joint one.....don't be afraid to jump in....the papers showed that some of you lean left and others right.....but most of you are down the middle.....so the necessary question is....knowing there are so many diverse views......can we work as a team? Can we do that without splintering?

ETHAN: Professor....I'm the conservative you alluded to....no reason to hide it....but I'm not one with a closed mind....or one that can't have coffee with Estelle......I know she's a whacky liberal, but she's also very pretty....that wipes away all hesitation.....so that helps......our goal is to get a man into congress with an intellect..... and, of course, you're the man we admire....

SARAH: I am so ready to spend the next year working for you.....and I still won't be able to vote for you in November....but I will also be there to work for and vote for your reelection in two years......[A MURMUR OF APPROVAL]

JAMES: Professor....I think that I pretty much speaks for everyone....we fully realize that trying to do this is not all flag waving and glory....it will require thousands of hours of hard work....much of it repetitive and drudgery....but it won't be all drudge....we'll laugh and we'll joke....we'll love the comradeship.....yet, we all believe that the real goal is not just the election, but the welfare of our nation....and with that in mind, how could our efforts not be worth it.?

GUY: James, ...you are scheduled to teach undergraduates next year......Alan, I've read their responses just as you have....and I hear our people speaking.... I know how moved you are by purity and willingness of their thoughts....honestly.....if I were in your shoes, with all you have to offer....I would run.....

ALAN: I'll have to take that under advisement.....but people ...I have to share this with you....the basic idea is from something I read in Norman Mailer or Steven Ambrose.....when, or if you go to war...there can only be one goal and generally one outcome....to win......anything less generally means death.....so every soldier must sublimate him or herself to the common goal....what we are looking for here is like war.....fortunately one without live ammunition....there must be one objective....personal sacrifice, in many ways, will be called for....disagreement on tactics or even politics, dare not fracture our army,....it would be disastrous....it calls for the self assurance to work with others, even when it doesn't suit you...your opportunity to bend things will come when the war is won...any less of a commitment and we would fail.....

7 - ONE ACT PLAYS

ESTELLE: Wasn't it Vince Lombardi, the football coach who said, "winning isn't everything, but losing is nothing"?

GUY: I believe you're right......

JAMES: How come you know so much about football?

ESTELLE: Have you met my brothers?...

JAMES: Now, I'm afraid to......

HERMAN: Professor.....even in war....there can be disagreements on tactics or on goals or anything

ALAN: That's true.....but it gets squared away quietly at company headquarters.....not everyone will be in total accord....but when the captain calls the shot.....we will all charge up the hill in the same direction...

MARY ELLEN: And if we can't possibly live with the direction prescribed?

ALAN: Then in such a circumstance and also not a live ammunition war.....the proper thing would be to drop out and not bad mouth the group.....

HAMILTON: I must say, young people....if this crab grass roots project were to work.....and it can....neither Guy nor Alan or myself have ever heard of such a thing.....

ALAN: You gave us almost fifty drafts to read.....that's a pretty good cross section......and then you tell us that the movement has added more than one hundred willing young workers in this one week......that's quite alive......

SARAH: It' so exciting.....it seems like one out of every two we approach is ready and anxious to participate.

ALAN: ready is easy....sustaining is hard....before we break...please understand that I, too, have been doing homework.....and I must outline some of the things we must commit to.....it's not simply making signs and collecting money.....there are more than two hundred households in our district....care to call out the ethnic diversity?

ESTELLE: I'll start with the Hispanic......

HERMAN: Asian....not all Chinese.....

LILLIAN: A lot of our farmers are from northern European backgrounds...

JOSEPH: hell, it's obvious....other parts of Europe....there's Africa, the Middle East.....

ETHAN: What about religions?

ALAN: Now you're getting it......we must make maps and color them....we must get known ethnic leaders behind our movement and use their input to reaching their people.....it's ethnic history, but pride in being an American, we'll have to visit every home, in pairs......let every family know you're interested in them....and care for them and their needs....each citizen must be treated with dignity, shown that they share a piece of the pie.....and most of all, you must believe it too, that you are an active baker of that pie....lastly, everyone who's positive must be listed in your book....and then you must get them out to vote...it isn't going to be easy.....

7 - ONE ACT PLAYS

JAMES: That's all professor? I thought you'd make it hard.....

ELAINE: Sounds like duck soup.....

COLIN: Duck soup is fatty....it'll give you a bellyache...

MARY ELLEN: There's our realist......

ALAN: And a good thing.....Okay....one more week....and no written homework this time....but a lot of thinking....this is a more than a one year project to election day....the first project is the primary we'll need signatures, honest ones......please return....whether you're positive or negative....you know the probable path in front of you and you're only the leaders....we will need many more foot soldiers.....I will do the same....I'm still not sure of my health...and whatever we decide next week....Professor Pearson will bring the coffee and donuts......

[THE GROUP BREAKS UP...STUDENTS LEAVE.... TALKING AS THEY GO....THE THREE PROFESSORS REMAIN]

ALAN: What do you think?

GUY: I'm glad you made me Gunga Din.....I'll bring the coffee......I'm sure they'll want it.....

HAMILTON: Alan, I have never been able to motivate a young group like you can...but I must give Guy the credit....he got them started on this road......

GUY: They came to me and it snowballed.....

HAMILTON: Alan, if you choose to run, I'll reduce your class load without loss of pay....The provost should be thrilled with the positive advertising and recognition the school will get.....even if you take a leave of absence....and it doesn't work out....your place is secure.....

ALAN: Ham,....if I run, I have no intention of losing....I'm not sure yet, but the competitive juices are flowing.....

GUY: Have you discussed this with Janet?

ALAN: Yeah....she thinks I should run....and she wants to get married....but I don't think I can do that to her.....

GUY: She's a big girl......and she's a smart girl....she knows what she wants.....trust me.....sex diminishes very rapidly after the honeymoon......it becomes less and less important...love is what lasts a lifetime....ask anyone...except Ruth Westheimer and Hugh Hefner....Alan...go home...it's not a simple decision......the kids may have made it easier, but that's only where the real work begins.

[LIGHTS DIM END OF SCENE]

[LIGHTS UP....SAME AS SCENE THREE JOHN AND ABBY'S LIVING ROOM PLUS TWO ADDED CHAIRS.....JOHN IS SEATED...ABBY IS PUTTING SOME FINISHING TOUCHES ON CANAPES FOR OTHER GUESTS]

JOHN: Do you think he'll go through with it?

ABBY: I don't know....and I don't even know what I wish for him....but he's never walked away from a challenge....the big

7 - ONE ACT PLAYS

one, they carried him out on a stretcher, not walking.....to be a congressman is such a wonderful accomplishment....and he'd be good at it....but I worry about his health...he's been through so much.....

JOHN: And Jan?

ABBY: She's such a terrific person....nothing's been concealed from her...and she's not a child....my brother's fortunate to have her.

[THE BELL RINGS....ENTER ALAN AND JAN CARRYING AN ORCHID ....HUGS AND KISSES.....JOHN RISES]

ABBY: [TAKING THE FLOWER]...Thank you darling....it's lovely....

JOHN: A drink anyone?

JANET: I think we'll wait for the wine with dinner...the hard stuff doesn't agree with either of us.....

JOHN: Well, have you two decided yet.?

JANET: Ask him I've proposed four times already....I even bought the ring....I'm still waiting for an answer......

ALAN: [JOKING]...I don't like to be rushed....

ABBY: You're a meathead...I'm going to make Jan my kid sister, whether you marry her or not.....

JOHN: Have you guys given much more thought to running?

JANET: Everything's in flux now.....Alan's thinking....the students are thinking......

ABBY: I'll tell you what I'm thinking....I'm thinking that my dopey baby brother, who always wanted to move mountains is dreaming of trying again.....

ALAN: Honey, I swear....I'm a realist....and if I were to give it all my energy....maybe I can move a small rock.....

ABBY: And with your luck, a big one will fall on top of your head....

ABBY: Darling, you volunteered as an officer after school.....the desert and the war took a whole portion of your life.....don't let your sense of honor take the rest...

ALAN: Enough of this fiddle faddle....what are you serving tonight?

ABBY: You'll find out when I put it in front of you....and remember...pretend to use your knife and fork this time...we have other guests

JOHN: Do you remember our friends Fred and Cathy? Fred's just signed on with Lambert labs....It's a huge jump in salary and responsibility over his last assignment.....

ALAN: Forensic engineer, if I remember right?

JANET: And a brilliant one....he's the expert that bailed Lambert out of a huge liability suit.....

7 - ONE ACT PLAYS

ABBY: He's very smart...but it's Cathy I like....she doesn't even hate bumble bees......{DOORBELL RINGS]

JOHN: [GOING TO THE DOOR] I'll get it...

ENTER FRED AND CATHY...FRED WITH A BOTTLE OF WINE...HE IS A BIG MAN.....SELF ASSURED.... CATHY...MIDDLE...THIRTIES..PLEASANT LOOKING...DEMURE...HUGS..KISSES...HELLOS.... FRED HANDS THE WINE TO ABBY

FRED: It's a fine Montrechet....already chilled....[HE TURNS TO ALAN}..so professor, how's the college? Flunk a half a class yet?

ALAN: Not really.....I either flunk the whole class or pass them all....after all, they've paid their tuition.....

FRED: Sounds liberal enough.....that's the advantage you have.... answers don't have to be specific.....everything's a judgment call on your part.....

ALAN: You know, when I was a freshman undergraduate I flipped a coin.....heads, physics....tails, philosophy....it took me three times before tails came up....anyway..congratulations on your new job....John told us about it.....

JANET: And I read your report on the Lambert case....very impressive...I'm putting your name in my book of expert experts....

FRED: Thank you.....

JOHN: [BRINGING IN AN OPEN BOTTLE OF WINE AND GLASSES} Wine everyone? and if you don't mind, help yourselves....Abby needs me.....[HE EXITS...JANET TAKES OVER AND POURS FOR EVERYONE...JUST A NOTED SMALL DROP FOR ALAN MAKING CONVERSATION]

JANET: Cathy, if I remember correctly, you were quite involved with our emerging city orchestra?

CATHY: Oh yes, it's really getting there....never be a philharmonic of course, but it's growing... and developing a pops style repertoire...much like the Boston Pops..

JANET: Sounds great...

CATHY: We are limited.....it's part time for everyone except our musical director......and now we're including top kids from the colleges and high schools....

FRED: Maybe these kids would be better served if they put that time into mathematics?

JOHN: [REENTERING] Nope...better basketball...our teams stink......[he gets a negative reaction from all the women] Okay, okay. I'm kidding......we're a small population...tough to compete.....

ALAN: That sounds like a copout...in many ways, we're a microcosm of the whole nation....if we and all others like us, do the best we can...all will follow..

JOHN: That almost sounds like a campaign speech.....

ALAN: Don't push it...nothing's decided yet....

7 - ONE ACT PLAYS

CATHY: How exciting....you're running for something?

ABBY: [ENTERING...PICKS UP HER GLASS OF WINE)... Many people would like Alan to run for congress.....

FRED: Against Blakely?....you'll never unseat him....he's too entrenched with the old guard.....

JANET: There's a new guard.....and then there's a lot of disillusioned old guard......

FRED: [AT ALAN] You're playing with yourself...[CATCHES HIMSELF] ..oh, I'm sorry...didn't quite mean -----

ALAN: It's all right Fred....no offense....I'm not that self conscious.....

FRED: Well, I'm no political expert, but you'd be asking a lot.....

ALAN: I know that....that's why no decisions have been made yet....

ABBY: [HER TURN TO MAKE CONVERSATION AND STEER IT AWAY FROM POLITICS] Cathy, with the new job for Fred, anything new on the horizon?

CATHY: Now, it is time to think about a family.....we've looked into that new community in Kenilworth....besides a beautiful four bedroom, two and a half bath home, it has lovely grounds...a community clubhouse and pool and playground....even the price is reasonable....

FRED: Everything but the mix....only seventy percent white.... the rest is a mix of minorities and other ethnics....I don't know if I can live with that.....

JANET: [HER BACK UP] Would you prefer it the other was around?

ALAN: Have you joined the twenty first century....or are you still living in the past?

FRED: Don't be a wise ass. What's the past have to do with it?

ALAN: Lily white isn't the majority any more....in a lot of places there's a variety of colors...like a flower bed....and so what....that house you want is going to cost you a half million dollars before your through.....don't you think that anyone who can afford that much for a home is worthy of your distinguished friendship?

FRED: It isn't that....

JANET: Then what is it?

FRED: I just won't be comfortable around them...neither would Cathy.....

JANET: Cathy, you feel that way too?

CATHY: No....not exactly....but if Fred's not happy, I won't be either....

ALAN: I can't believe what I'm hearing......

JOHN: Slow down Alan.......not everyone has your point of view...Man...you've written advertising copy....you know we aim to specific targets....money, age, religion, even race....they all call for different approaches in many things....hell, we don't educate...we stimulate....

7 - ONE ACT PLAYS

JANET: Well guys....I hope you know how to change your aim as your targets diffuse....half the marriages today are either inter religious or bi racial.....soon we'll all be of the same color....

ABBY: [TRYING TO LIGHTEN THINGS] That'll certainly screw up profiling at airports....soon they'll have to pat down everyone......

ALAN: I've slowed down....but we're off the point....

ALAN: That separate but equal doesn't exist....and had you been in Iraq as I was...you'd be very aware that blood flows red from every wound....and that every man Jack that was at my side....was there to protect you and your new home....

ABBY: [INTERRUPTING] Dinner's ready....everyone...to the dining room where your mouth will be too full to speak

[LIGHTS DIM...ALL EXIT STAGE...END OF SCENE]

[OPEN SCENE SIX...SAME AS SCENE FOUR....ONLY GUY ALAN AND HAMILTON ARE ON STAGE....GUY HAS THE COFFEE AND DONUTS ON THE TABLE]

GUY: The students should be here shortly....they were talking about bringing reinforcements......

HAMILTON: I know they are....they've been talking about nothing else all week....

ALAN: Do you think they really understand the commitment to be made? Hell, we don't even know what we're letting ourselves in for?

HAMILTON: Alan, in all my years, I've never seen a ground swell like this…it's even louder than the demand I remember for coed dorms!….

ALAN: You know, I faced combat only a short time before I was hit…But I learned a hell of a lot in that short time…we had a surprising ethnic mix in my small platoon….and when we dug into the ground, the sand covered our faces…we were all the same color….and all ready to die for each other……how can I translate that lesson to others….and to this mission?

GUY: I haven't an answer for you…..but you do reach these young people ..and you'll know how to reach everyone….but you may have to talk to everyone before you're done……

ALAN: I spoke to someone two nights ago and struck out……

HAMILTON: Maybe you planted a seed and don't know it…..

ALAN: I doubt it….my sister shut him up with mashed potatoes….

GUY: Alan, do you even know if you want to do this?

ALAN: I'm still not one hundred percent…but this idiot may have planted a seed in me…..

HAMILTON: Hooray for mashed potatoes

[THE STUDENTS FILE IN…ANIMATED….SOME SIT SOME STAND…HAPPY GREETINGS ALL AROUND.]

GUY: Good morning everyone….hope that you slept well….no classes this morning…..they would be easier than what we are contemplating….

7 - ONE ACT PLAYS

JAMES: I don't think any of us have had much sleep all week.....by the way, our district is a little over four hundred fifty thousand people.....I don't exactly know how many eligible voters, but I'd guess about three hundred....

MARY ELLEN: According to the records....in the last presidential election. The actual vote count was one hundred thirty thousand, three hundred twelve....almost a sixty forty break down for Blalkely....that's a hell of a challlenge...

COLIN: That's right along party lines......

LILLIAN: That would work for us......first we have to unseat Blakely in the primary......once we do that....the party affiliation will work for us....especially when we add new voters...Obama did it on the internet......we're all savvy...

COLIN: Then we're going after him in the primary?

JAMES: Without a doubt...even if we had to go third party....Even if w go independent....we'll get plenty of signatures easily....first step anyway

ETHAN: I've done a lot od talking this week....and specifically with adults over fifty.....most of them know Blakely....he's a good guy....they know him

ESTELLE: Sure he is...but that a tough part of the job we have....he's not a bad man...but he's yesterday....we have to convince these middles and seniors to worry about their children and grandchildren

LILLIAN: We should talk to them too....like on TV....kids talk to their parents, especially when they're motivated....

SARAH: Right, that's our job.....to get out the vote and make the professor look like he walks on water.....

HERMAN: No, we have to make him real....real to everyone....a son....a brother....an accessible right arm.....

JAMES: He's also a war hero....everyone will want to identify with him.....

ALAN: No....no hero...simply a veteran....you don't want to sell me as a soldier....people must see me as thinking human being with an intellect and two ears....who listens...

GUY: The modesty will become you.....the silver star story will come out anyway.....

JAMES: A number of us have given thought to money....maybe no big donors...but if we could average two bucks a voter, we'll have plenty....especially since we're not getting paid.....

ETHAN: Professor Pearson guarantees at least three credits in poly/sci...that's worth something...if we're not getting paid

MARY ELLEN: Not for seniors...we're out of here!!

GUY: We didn't forget you....credit, if you stay for graduate studies....or a letter commendation to you next school or employer...

COLIN: With my luck, I'll get a job with a man who hates politics...you never taught us anarchy, professor.........

7 - ONE ACT PLAYS

HERMAN: Hey guys....hold on for a minute....everybody sounds up high...a little like Micky Rooney and Judy Garland saying "Let's make a musical." one reel later the barn's ready and everyone is singing.....We can't build a barn in one or in one month....we can't do it with fancy talk.....are we ready for the war the professor spoke of last week?

ALAN: [INTERRUPTING] My turn...I'm impressed by how you're approaching this....you really care......but Herman is right......are we sincerely ready to go to war?....And, in truth, I'm still on the fence......a little scared if you will?

ELAINE: Scared?

ALAN: Oh yes.....scared.....anyone who goes to war....bullets or no....and isn't scared.....is either fooling himself or stupid....the hills of this world are filled with the bodies who ran headlong forward without proper preparation....again....we must ask ourselves....are we prepared?....prepared for all the work? And to see failure as not an option....

JAMES: I believe we are, professor!

ALAN: Okay, I'll tell you what.....one lat time ....let's each retire to our own caucus for for a few days....you, as a group....me, with Guy and Hamilton....and lrt me paraphrase Arthur Miller.... "In politics, what you see or think you see. Is rarely what you get" We should each return with a positive or negative answer....if it's negative, I'll be here next year to evaluate your term papers......If it's a double positive.....you can start calling me Alan.....

DIM LIGHTS....END OF PLAY

TROOP SHIP

Written by Jerry "Josh" Konsker

written: 1958

[CAST OF CHARACTERS]

STAFF SGT. BIILEM Late 20s........combat veteran....served in WWII and an earlier tour in Korea.....H.S. graduate...drafted at 18........married and divorced.

HOBIE Small town 18 year old enlistee.....average intelligence....H.S. grad.

VIC A year or two of college, but left school and enlisted...... friendly, stoic, figures that he'll find a way out of the infantry

EDDIE 20 year old draftee.......opportunist.....small....smart..... very scared although to outside world would put up a brave front

CHICO 19 Hispanic from the lower east side of the Bronx..... only child of single mother......frightened of the unknown......lacks self-confidence despite that the army has helped him to grow

** Please note: *This story is based upon the true events that occurred on a "troop ship" that was carrying more than four thousand newly trained infantry men to Korea in May 1953. This play was written*

and director by Jerry "Josh" Konsker while attending Adelphi University after the Korean War had ended. Jerry attended and graduated from Adelphi University in 1958 with the assistance of the GI Bill.

[SETTING: THE TIME IS EARLY SPRING OF 1953..... STANDARD TYPE TROOP SHIP IS CROSSING THE PACIFIC OCEAN ON IT'S WAY TO JAPAN AND KOREA CARRYING AS MANY AS 5000 MEN].

[SCENE IS A HOLD OF THE SHIP THAT WAS CONVERTED TO SLEEPING QUARTERS. THE BACK AND SIDE WALLS ARE WHITE PAINTED ROWS OF SEA BUNKS....EACH PILED FOUR HIGH....TWO REAL BUNKS ARE ON EITHER SIDE ON THE FLOOR LEVEL BEING PREPARED FOR INSPECTION. THE FLOOR IS LITTERED WITH PAPER AND OTHER DEBRIS OF MEN LIVING IN VERY CRAMPED QUARTERS..... THERE ARE BROOMS AND MOPS PLUS OTHER CLEANING MATERIALS ARE ON SET. FOUR MEN ARE SEEN ON STAGE..HOBIE IS SEATED ON THE FLOOR PLAYING SOLITAIRE......EDDIE IS ALONE BY HIS BUNK LOOKING FOR SOMETHING HIDDEN...CHICO A DARK, POWERFUL AND INTENSIVE LOOKING MAN IS UPSTAGE WITH VIC WHO IS FAIRER AND A LESS STRIKING FIGURE. THEY TOO, ARE ADJUSTING THEIR GEAR FOR INSPECTION.]

[SGT. GILLEM ENTERS STAGE LEFT]

SGT: What the hell is this mess....inspection in 45 minutes....if you fail, you gonna stay in this shithole without a break for the whole three days until we get off this ship....I'm going topside for

7 - ONE ACT PLAYS

a half hour....I'm also disappearing.... Fail and I don't know you... let them find me.......you got a half hour.....

HOBIE: Hey sarge.....don't understand it.....I eat everything they give me and a thousand of those little pills....but when this ship starts rollin', I swear my insides was swimmin'.

SGT: Maybe your stomach's too big to follow the rules.....we ain't all sailors.

HOBIE: Man you ain't just kidding.....when we get off this tub in three days, I'll be one of the happiest men alive....we ain't goin' anyplace good, but at least I'll have some solid ground under me. [PENSIVE FOR A MOMENT].   ...**Hey Sarge!!?**.....

SGT: Yeah?

HOBIE: What's it really like?...over there in Korea, I mean?.... What are they talkin' about with these hoomin sea attacks....I don't remember ever seein nothin' like that in the movies......

SGT: It's not in the movies, Hobie, It's real and it's different....the Chinese got a whole bunch of kids....not soldiers.....and they got them all hopped up on opium.....and in sloppy uniforms....thye even got some north Korean kids mixed in.... When the attack starts, these kids come first.....they ain't got no weapons....some just sticks.....We burn out our machine guns and rifles...run out of ammunition.....and then we gotta retreat or get reenforcements..... but now I think we're ready for them better.......fresh guns and ammo are moved right into position.....also we use some light artillery to blow them all apart.....we're pretty good soldiers [HESITATING....AS IF SUDDENLY REMEMBERING SOMETHING SPECIFIC] That depends.....

HOBIE: [SLOWLY...TRYING TO UNDERSTAND ALL THAT'S JUST BEEN SAID] depends? Depends on what?

SGT: What kind of person you are.....it's a terrible sight.....killing all those kids ...even if they are in those phony uniforms......it's a sad sight.....and a worse feeling....well, I guess it's sorta on who you are and how you think about things [HE WOULD LIKE TO END THIS DISCUSSION] You will learn....we all do......

HOBIE: Yeah, but the shit we hear....the reports and stuff..... they true, ain't they?

SGT: They're not too far from wrong....[HIS PATIENCE EBBING] it gets messy sometimes.

CHICO: [WHO HAS BEEN LISTENING INTENTLY TO THE PAIR SUDDENLY DROPS HIS SHAVING MUG TO THE FLOOR...TO HIM IT SOUNDS LIKE THE HAMMERS OF HELL HE POUNCES ON IT LIKE A CAT]

Son of a bitch!!

[AS HE PICKS IT UP, HE REALIZES THAT EVERYONE IS LOOKING AT HIM...HE TURNS SLOWLY TO HIS BUNK]

VIC: [SLIPS OVER TO CHICO].. Hey man, what's the matter?....you losing it?

CHICO: What? No....no

VIC: You're sure acting like it......

7 - ONE ACT PLAYS

CHICO: [BREAKING SUDDENLY] Christ Vic, ...I don't know what to do....it's been two nights since I got any real sleep....ever since we started hearing about the heavy casualties and human sea attacks.....I ain't eating right and that makes the nausea worse.....

VIC: Look kid, calm down.....where's you Chicano blood.....I always heard that Chicanos were tough guys.....Besides....there's no guarantee as to exactly where we're heading....and those reports are scuttle but anyway......

CHICO: [RELAXING A LITTLE] This Chicano's from the tribe of lovers...I wish I could feel the way you do....but then I'd be lying to myself....just like you are....

VIC: No argument there kid, but just take it a little slower....don't go looking for trouble....it'll come to you fast enough.....

CHICO: Yeah....you know Vic,......all my life, I wanted to do something decent with my life, and now the whole thing wants to blow up in my face...

SGT: [HAS COME OVER TO WHERE THE TWO ARE TALKING] Trouble?

VIC: No trouble Sarge....we're just both upset some....you know....about the war and all....

SGT: So What....there ain't a man on this ship who isn't.....you ain't special.....

CHICO: Yeah,....but a guy should be able to control himself.....I feel like I want to hit somebody...then I'll be sorry....

SGT: So don't hit nobody....look, Chico....everybody's different....this is the third time I'm heading for it.....once in the last war and once here.....It ain't any easier......I'm just more used to it....

CHICO: [INTERRUPING] Yeah....but

SGT: Just let me finish, before you say anything else {HOBIE IS NOW SITTTING ON THE EDGE OF HIS BUNK READING A COMIC BOOK] LOOK AT Hobie there.....you think nothing bothers him?...try shouting at him, ...he'll jump like you hit him with a hot poker....he's as tight a you are....he just shows it different....even Eddie would be a damn sight easier to live with if he wasn't so screwed up inside......I ain't traveled with you guys so that I don't know him long.....but he's a prick....I know one when I see one....don't buddy up with him....if you wind up in the same outfit......he'll get you killed......

CHICO: I know you're right Sarge....I just wish I didn't feel like running away from it all.....

HOBIE: [SENSES THAT THE OTHERS ARE TALKING ABOUT HIM, PUTS THE BOOK ASIDE} hey sarge, we have to clean the latrine again today?

SGT: Yep. Same as you did yesterday and the day before that....

EDDIE: When's our turn to get a break?

SGT: You gonna start that again? three days...you're off this ship.....

EDDIE: [MIMICKING HIM] Yeah, I'm gonna start that again......stilll don't know why we should be down this hole pullin' all the details....all the others are up on deck eating oranges....why, in hell, can't the navy clean their own lousy ships?

SGT: [ANNOYED] cause you're so good at it....[AS HE EXITS] just get it done!!

EDDIE: All I know is that if you guys left things to me, I'd get us off this shit ass detail....there's too many guys laying around with nothing to do, while we play janitor..........

VIC: if it's not us, it'll be four others...

EDDIE: At least it'll be them and not us....

HOBIE: C'mon....stop arguing" ....the man's right....let's just get to it....Besides, time passes better when you're doin' somthin'

VIC: Okay Hobie, you called it.....

HOBIE: Chico, you can have the broom....I'm takin' the mop... gonna make believe it's a woman with stringy hair so I can sing to her you'll see Chico. Time passes quick....

VIC: That mop's all the woman you're gonna see for a long time.... at least till your first R &R....the little Japanese girls are gonna be more than you can handle

HOBIE: I know they got ladies in Korea, don't they....man don't you ever think that this little southern boy ain't been around he'll hold his own....[THE SGT RE-ENTERS] Hey Sarge, what happens when we get to that Sasebo place?

SGT: Don't you remember nothing"....same thing I told you yesterday....off this ship.... You go to a big Quonset hut....give up your class A uniforms....get new fatigues....extra underwear and socks.....get your back pack...sleeping gear, bayonet, shovel, soap, shavers, and anything else they can think of....then you get your rifle, memorize the serial number, out on the firing range and zero it in....then back on another ship....goes overnight to Inchon.....

HOBIE: More time on a ship?

SGT: Only a day or so....probably go down the ropes at Inchon, into a landing craft and to shore.....

HOBIE: We gonna see shooting there?

SGT: I don't know....I don't think so.....

HOBIE: Shit!!

CHICO: [TRYING TO CHANGE THE SUBJECT] Sarge, what time is inspection?

HOBIE: [NOT RELENTING] and then?

SGT: You now,....you're like a little baby...I gotta keep repeating the same thing till it gets in your thick skull.....

HOBBIE: Yeah,....but.....

SGT: Okay, okay.....They'll split us all up....you'll be assigned to a division and a regiment and a company.....God only knows what some CO will do with you....well, if you're still alive after the first month, you'll probably make it all the way.....

HOBIE: So, how do you do that?....stay alive, I mean?

7 - ONE ACT PLAYS

EDDIE: Keep your head down stupid......

HOBIE: Nobody asked you, ass hole..!!...

SGT: Get off him Ed....we'll see how smart you are when the shooting starts.......that's enough now.....we're all infantry and we know where we're going....now....get this place cleaned up for inspection and you can get out of this hole for the rest of the day...{SARGE EXITS]

EDDIE: [SLIPPING OVER NEAR CHICO} There's lots of guys never go near the front line....all they gotta do is be smart.....

HOBIE: Some times, you're too smart for your own good, college boy.....any body got a cigarette?

CHICO: [FISHING IN HIS POCKET} Christ don't you ever carry your own....

HOBIE: Don't have to....I got you....besides, they cost too much.....

CHICO: I'm gonna kick your ass...they're a dime a pack at the PX.....

[ANNOUNCEMENT OVER THE LOUDSPEAKER]

[NOW HEAR THIS.....NOW HEAR THIS...ALL SWEEPERS MAN YOUR BROOMS AND MOPS...WASH DOWN FORE AND AFT....INSPECTION IN THIRTY MINUTES]

VIC: [TAKING CHARGE] Well, you heard the man.....we better get to work....

ED: Who, the fuck, put you in charge?

CHICO: [A TOUGH KID WHEN HE WANTS TO BE] Cool it....we got a job to do....let's just do it....

[ED MOVES UPSTAGE....HOBIE OFF TO LEFT..... LEAVING VIC AND CHICO ALONE CENTER].

VIC: [TEASING CHICO] You're kind of quiet for a big man.... did they draft you out of elementary school?

CHICO: Man, what did you learn in college? there's a whole world of people you know nothin' about.....

VIC: Sorry....I didn't mean anything...you're really a nice kid..... one I could be buddies with....so don't get mad....

CHICO: That's okay....you're an all right guy.....No, I wasn't drafted....I enlisted....I got out of high school okay, but the only way I'd get to college is the GI bill....and I promised my mom that I'd go to school and take care of her when I got back......I didn't think I'd wind up here......not smart, huh?

VIC: If you're scared?....we all are......

CHICO: A little, yeah....It's just that she took care of me, all alone.....and I swore I'd take care of her.....now, I gotta worry if I'm even coming back....who's gonna help her? She's getting old and sick.....

VIC: Where's your old man?

7 - ONE ACT PLAYS

CHICO: That's a good question....he thought he was a God damn Bumble bee.. You know, goin' from flower to flower and makin' a deposit......my mom thinks she knows who it was..

VIC: Oh sorry, I didn't mean to pry....

CHICO: Don't matter....I don't know him......he's nothin' to me..... hey Vic,......later, if we get a chance to talk....I want to talk to you some more. Huh? [ED IS IN A POSITION TO OVERHEAR THIS STATEMENT}.

VIC: Sure thing kid any time......[AS HE GOES UPSTAGE] I'll clean the latrine with Hobie......there's some junk on my bunk...... straighten it out, will you?

[CHICO NODS OKAY TO VIC...GRABS A BROOM AND STARTS TO SWEEP THE FLOORS].

ED: [TRYING TO BE FRIENDLY] If you take the floors, I'll do the walls and bunks.

CHICO: Okay

ED: I figure it'll be easier that way.....

CHICO: Doesn't matter

ED: You know.... I heard that some ships take the southern route....they can take twenty days to reach Japan [CHICO ISN'Y PAYING ATTENTION TO HIM] it all goes as overseas time also [STILL NO RESPONSE] You know the trouble with this army......they don't know how to take care of their men....

CHICO: What are you talkin' about?

ED: Take the British, for instance....I read a lot of books about their soldiers all over the world.....they allow women to follow the troops....

CHICO: No shit?...but I hear they make sweet guys like you one of the girls......

ED: Even in Korea....they hire young girls to stay in the tents and keep the place clean and all....of course they do one or two other things.....

CHICO: [ANNOYED] So what?

ED: so that's the kind of set up I'd like to have......just me....and some tender little Korean lass...

CHICO: So why the hell didn't you join the British army?.... You're as useful as tits on a bull here......

ED: What's that supposed to mean?

CHICO: It means that it takes a big man to make it with a sixteen year old kid

[ED TRIES TO RETORT, BUT CHICO GIVES HIM NO ENCOURAGEMENT AND TURNS HIS BACK....ED REACHES BEHIND A BUNK AND THROWS OUT A BUNCH OF ORANGE PEELS TO THE FLOOR]

ED: Filthy bastards....too damn lazy to throw their crap in a can.... we have to clean up their lousy garbage....why in_____

CHICO: Will you shut up and stop bitchin'....you ain't gonna change the world..

ED: Yeah,...I'll keep quiet....but how in hell do guys get so God damn dirty?

CHICO: I don't know....I only work here.....

ED: [TRYING TO BE A FRIEND] I didn't mean to blow up..... it's just that some times I can't stand this fucking job.....

CHICO: Nobody like it any more than you do......but we gotta do it.....

ED: [SUDDENLY] Chico,....how'd you like to get out of this mess?

ED: I'm not talking about this lousy detail....I'm talking about where we're going.....I know how we can stay in Japan and maybe never get to see Korea!!

CHICO: You're off you fucking nut...nobody leaves this barge in Japan except to get combat gear....and you know it...you heard the sarge...now lay off...[HE TURNS HIS BACK ON ED AND WALKS AWAY]

ED: But....[HE SEES CHICO'S BACK TO HIM AND RETURNS TO WORK....GIVING UP...THEN HE LOOKS AT CHICO AGAIN] Chico [CHICO DOESN'T REPLY]... Chico...what was it you wanted to talk to Vic about?

CHICO: First of all....it's none of your business.....second...it's nothing ....just something about some schools....

ED: Hell,....why not ask me?..... spent some time in college...I'd be glad to help.....

CHICO: Forget it....it wasn't important.....

ED: ANGRILY] What am I? horseshit?....doesn't anybody loosen up a little here?[[Chico turns away again}...That's it....turn your back on me....I go out of my way to be nice and you turn your back.....go to Vic for advice....nobody else went to college or knows anything......

CHICO: [SOFTENED] look, Ed,...I----------

ED: [PRESSING IT NOW] You're all the same....even an ox like Hobie wouldn't listen when I tried to explain a poker rule... one that any jackass could understand....I had a way to get us off this detail and everyone jumped on me for it.....and now I want to help with something very important to you....and you freeze me out.....

CHICO: All right....I didn't mean to be nasty Ed,...it's only that---------------

ED: Yeah....I know....but I figured you and I could talk....you know you and I got a lot in common....neither of wants to go where we're headed....and we both got a lot of plans for when we get out....

CHICO: That's great....but first we gotta get out in one piece......

ED: We can do that too....when you're a loner like me, you learn to take care of yourself....shit, in basic I pulled a phony leg injury and got a desk job for the last eight weeks.....

CHICO: That gimmick may have worked nice in basic.....but it won't do you much good in where we're going.....

ED: That's right...it won't do no good in a line company....if we get that far....we'll be in real trouble....so I ain't planning to get that far......

CHICO: Now you're talking crazy.....

ED: This ain't crazy talk....it's scared talk...and I'm just scared enough to do something desperate....Hey look....I learned something when I was a little kid...if a stove is hot?...don't touch it....this war is hot.....so I ain't gonna touch it either....

CHICO: you know...you're fucking stupid.....

ED: not too stupid to think......and just stupid enough to figure a way to get us out of this place.....we have a terrible accident.....a few broken bones....and we get carried off this ship in Japan..... but I need a partner....I can't do it alone.....

CHICO: Where the hell do you expect to find someone to go along with that asshole idea?

ED: That's easy....all I have to do is find someone as dumb or as smart as I am.....but I tell you something better.... I already found him.....

CHICO: Who?

ED: You....you schmuck...you're as scared as I am

CHICO: [COMPLETELY UPSET....ED STRUCK A NERVE] you're nuts...I may be scared, but I ain't crazy.....

ED: Bullshit....you haven't slept in four nights....so you gotta be held apart....

CHICO: How the fuck would you know?

ED: Cause I'm up all night too....asshole....

CHICO: You're outta your head....I don't-----

ED: Don't say no to me, cause we both know better.....you can't even try to kid me....I heard what you said to Vic.....It's been like this ever since we got those casualty reports.....you can't sit skill.... you got bugs in your head....too scared to eat right....

CHICO: Shut up......

ED: [GOING ON] And now you're worried there ain't no future....a man can't live without a future to to plan on.....and you're too screwed up to think you still have a plan.....ain't you?

CHICO: I said shut up!!

ED: No future...no present...nothing...too scared...ain't you....

CHICO: You want me to kill you?....sure I'm scared....that's what you want to hear? You feel better now???

[CHICO GRABS ED BY THE LAPELS AND DRAWS HIM CLOSE...ALMOST LIFTING HIM OFF THE GROUND.... ED IS TERRIFIED.....CHICO RELAXES AND LETS HIM FALL AWAY..CHICO TURNS AWAY AND TALKS TO HIMSELF] you're right, I'm not fooling anyone....I'll wind up loading trucks like all the idiots on my block if I even get back to the block.....

ED: [GAINING LIFE] Chico, if you'd-----------

7 - ONE ACT PLAYS

CHICO: [GOING ON] Christ, maybe I'm not even that lucky [FEELING SORRY FOR HIMSELF] I'll probably get my head blown off on some shit ass hill......or maybe a hunk of steel in my gut so I can eat mush the rest of my life...even that would be a miracle....-------

ED: That's what I've been trying to tell you ass hole....you don't need miracle....just a small break...

CHICO: Are you still on that crap?

ED: I never left it........and if you'd shut your God damned mouth for a minute and listen....you'd find out....I got a plan to get us taken off this ship at Sasebo and taken to a hospital...while every one else goes on to Inchon....

CHICO: Your mouth is still running....

ED: It never stopped......I've got the whole thing figured.....but I need your help

CHICO: Why me?

ED: I don't give a damn who it is I tried myself....but it takes two guys to pull it off....and man, you're the right one....so tell me, do you want to play boy hero. Or get off this lousy ship......well, do you want off or not??

CHICO: Yeah, damn you....

ED: All tight then...now sit down and listen while I give you the whole bit....and don't interrupt until I'm done....now, two things we better get squared away real quick....if you're in this, you have to do what I say and second, nobody hears else hears about it, especially your friend Vic....the whole thing is so easy, it's ridiculous....and I know of a lot of guys who got reassigned in Japan and never even smelled Korea...either real sick or hurt is the only way it works.....I don't know how to get sick, so that means hurt....and the way this ship's been rolling the last few days....a few accidents won't seem odd......

CHICO: But---------------

ED: No one's gonna be surprised if two guys fell down a stairwell....especially the steep on by the storeroom..[ED GOES TO HIS BUNK AND PULLS OUT A ONE FOOT PIECE OF STEEL PIPE] we take this pipe.....you use it to break my arm...then we go to the top of the stairs where I'll use it to crack your ankle....we wait for a lurch and down we go....bruises, busted bones and all....no one would ever suspect

CHICO: What do you do with the pipe?

ED: It fits into the handle of the doorway by the storeroom....look kid...the war's supposed to be over in a few months...that's all the delay we need....Eisenhower said so.....

CHICO: The whole thing's so crazy....you must be kidding me ...it ain't gonna work

ED: It got to work....it will work...I got the whole thing figured out!

CHICO: The why don't you do it yourself?

7 - ONE ACT PLAYS

ED: Because I can't break my own arm...someone's got to do it for me...

CHICO: [LOOKING FOR A WAY TO BACK OUT} Are you sure you know how to break a leg?

ED: I told you....with the pipe it will be quick and clean....all you have to do is twist the ankle and the put the sudden pressure on it....even a light tap will break it.....you shove a hanker chief in your mouth and it'll muffle your voice when you get hit.....now, will you do it Chico?....no one will hear us....will you do it? CHICO [TRYING TO ANSWER AND CAN'T....FINALLY BLURT OUT], I don't know....don't know....your plan has too many holes in it...you'll get caught.....

ED: I won't get caught.....if I keep my mouth shut and follow the plan....

CHICO: That's no guarantee....don't you think the doctors will be smart enough to know what kind of bone breaks you'll have... they're too clean.....and the navy or army detectives...especially after they find the pipe.....

ED: Even if they do find out....we're better off....the worst they can do is give us a dishonorable discharge and six months in the stockade.....but we'll be alive and out of it....

CHICO: You'll never be out of it....you might as well be an ex convict.....a dishonorable means no money...no school....no nothing....no...the whole thing's wrong....we ain't supposed to do things this way....you ain't thinking right.....just like I told you.....

ED: People can do anything they can if it gets them what they want and need.....be honest with yourself....does anyone give a damn what happens to you? Will anybody give a shit if you make it to a line company? No...and you know it!

CHICO: Yeah...but-------

ED: No buts....if you go through with it, I swear I'll take care of you.....you know my old man's got a big business.....there's plenty of money there...I'll get you more money than the government would ever hand out.....I'll even get you a great job....you can go to school night or day.....but you won't sweat the money.....you've got to do this....for yourself....

CHICO: It ain't right.....it ain't right.....I'm scared, but I ain't no coward.....I ain't a girl in a man's body.....go find some other jerk...I won't turn you in..but you'll get caught....I'll send you candy in jail........If you get me hooked into your lousy plan, I'll kill you.... with my bared hands..

[THEY ARE INTERRUPTED BY THE CLANG OF STEEL BEING DROPPED ON THE DECK AND THE SOUND OF VOICE COMING FROM THE LATRINE.... ED AND CHICO BREAK AWAY FROM EACH OTHER.... HOBIE ENTERS FIRST....HE IS FOLLOWED BY VIC AND SGT WHO ARE LIGHTING CIGARETTES]....

HOBIE: Man, what a stink in that place.....looks like everythin' eatin' yesterday was given back last night......couldn't take it no more without a break.....

7 - ONE ACT PLAYS

SGT: Might as well slow down a little....if you finish too fast they'll give you something else to do....relax, I'll be back in awhile...[HE EXITS]

HOBIE: You know, another night like last night and they'll be sleeping in the latrine........big wave and no one in their bunks....got a cigarette for me Chico?

CHICO: If you don't get your own, I'm going to put one in your ass and light it.....[HE TAKES ONE FOR HIMSELF AND GIVES ONE TO HOBIE]

HOBIE: Can I help you light yours. I have my own lighter..... [WITH THAT, HOBIE BACKES UP QUICKLY SO CHICO CAN'T HIT HIM VIC WALKS OVER TO CHICO

VIC: You okay, kid....

CHICO: Sure I am....why wouldn't I be?

VIC: No reason....

CHICO: Well, ..I'm all right.....

VIC: You don't look so good.....are you sick?...your face is all red....

CHICO: That's not it....my stomach's acting up a little I think it must have been those powdered eggs this morning....They must have used sawdust too add to the amount.

VIC: If you want, I'll get you some dramamime pills from my

CHICO: I don't need any....and lay off me....don't ask so many God damn questions......I can take care of myself.....

VIC: TURNING AWAY] Okay, if that's the way you feel, I might as------

CHICO: No...don't go....I'm sorry ....I didn't mean to say that.... sit down, will ya Vic?

VIC: [SEATING HIMSELF SLOWLY AND STARING AT CHICO] Whatever you say kid....just settle yourself down....

CHICO: I'm sorry Vic...I didn't mean to jump at you like that.... sometimes a guy says things he didn't mean to say....they just come out....

VIC: It's okay....I understand...just forget it....talk about something else.....

CHICO: Yeah,...that's it let's forget it...talk about something else....

VIC: What was it you wanted to talk about before... probably school again....[CHICO LOOKS AT HIM...NOT COMPREHENDING FOR A MOMENT] Chico....before we started to work?

CHICO: [CALMER, BUT INTENSE] Vic, a guy can't get very far in this world without a decent education,......right?....especially without a family to back him up....right?

VIC: I'm afraid it is.....

7 - ONE ACT PLAYS

CHICO: And no way he can start a business, even a small one, without a chunk of cash?

VIC: Unless he gets some kind of screwy break....

CHICO: What do you mean?

VIC: I don't know exactly.......I guess it would have to be like one of those rich uncle stories, where somebody dies and leaves you a million dollars......but you ain't got an uncle like that....that's the movies.....there aren't too many of them around...and when they are.....it's always somebody else's uncle.....

CHICO: [HALF UNDER HIS BREATH] So you load trucks instead]

VIC: What?

CHICO: Nothing...I was just thikin' aloud....ain't a hell of a lot a guy can do about it......

VIC: Hey, ...it ain't as bad as all that.....I was thinking.....there's gotta be a few Chicano girls that are good looking, aren't there?

CHICO: you better believe it!!

VIC: Some of them must have fathers with money, or a good business that needs a smart young man.....but it does mean that you'll have to work damn hard to prepare yourself.....we'll get the GI bill, but it won't cover everything.....we'll have to work part time too....that ain't so bad....then be ready if the breaks come your way....it's like making your own breaks......

CHICO: And what if you get a break when you don't expect it?

VIC: Well, then you'd be a fool not to take advantage of it....

CHICO: Even though you may be screwing someone else?

VIC: Depends on how bad you're screwing him...

CHICO: To save your own life and let someone alse die in your... place?

VIC: Chico, you're getting way ahead of yourself.....we're not ready for that shit....

CHICO: And if we are.....what then?

VIC: You gotta take care of yourself first.....

CHICO: [CYNICAL BUT REFLECTIVE] It'd funny, all the things I think about....you get into a school, somebody else gets cut out......you get a job....someone else is outta work...you get the raise, some kid don't get a bike for Christmas. Are those the breaks we're talking about?

VIC: Now you're really in left field...you don't understand.....

CHICO: Maybe I understand too much....when your buddy gets a bullet in his belly.....you cry for him....but deep down inside, you're glad it's him laying there and not you.....so what's right?.... even when you're right, you're wrong

VIC: [GETTING AGGRESSIVE] Kid you're all jerked up.....sit down and listen....sure a guy has to take care of himself.....you're offered a million dollars, you don't turn it down cause you're the only one getting it....if you're lucky enough to get a rear echelon job, you gracefully smile and say thank you....you gotta do what's best for you...as long as you're not directly hurting someone else.....

CHICO: As long as it only affects you?.....then it's all right?

VIC: Yeah,......that's about it......

SGT: [RETURNING} That's enough talk for now....let's get this job finished..

HOBIE: [RISING] You mean we get to go back to the hole....boy are we lucky..

VIC: [TO HOBIE] I'll be with you in a second....[TO CHICO] Now, take it easy and...don't worry so much...you're a big boy now....[HE EXITS]

SGT: [FROM NEAR THE EXIT] We're running low on soap....get some from the store room like I told you....[EXITS]

ED: [LOOKS SLOWLY AT CHICO...HE HAS TAKEN THE PIECE OF PIPE FROM HIS BUNK AND HOLDS IT IN HIS HAND]...You heard the sarge......

CHICO: Yeah,....I heard him.....

ED: This is perfect....we have to go to the storeroom for soap.....

CHICO: Now?

ED: Now's the best time ...we're told to go...it'll look better....remember there's only three more days till Japan....and the ship is rollin'.....

CHICO: Maybe a little later

ED: No!! ...There is no later....let's go over the plan once more.... you use this pipe on my arm.....we go to the stairs by the store room...wait for a sudden lurch and the tumble down the stairs...I use the pipe on your ankle....we hide the pipe......and then scream for help....now....you got that Straight?...Chico....are you listening to me?

CHICO: [SLOWLY NODDING YES]

ED: Do you remember what I said about the gag in your mouth?......Damn it...look at me......your acting like you don't want to go through with it.....

CHICO: I don't know.....

ED: What do you mean, you don't know.....you have to know.... if we don't do it now we may never get another chance......now let's get started.......

CHICO: I can't get started....get that through your thick skull......

ED: But you want....you know you want to.....

CHICO: Yeah...yeah....I want to....but I don't know if I want to.....

ED: Bullshit ....take the pipe [CHICO TAKES THE PIPE] when I turn my elbow swing....now.....now......now I said.....

CHICO: All right....just shut up.....

ED: Now damn you....hit me.....

7 - ONE ACT PLAYS

CHICO: {struggling with himself] I can't.....I can't do it.....

ED: You've got to......you can't pull out now......use the damn pipe.....

CHICO: [BREAKING] I can't do it....[HE LETS THE PIPE DROP TO THE FLOOR AND JUST STANDS THERE WITHOUT MOVING...IT MAKES A LOUD NOISE]

ED: [CRYING WITH EMOTION]....You bastard....you yellow lousy rotten bastard!!!!

CHICO: [SUDDENLY LASHES OUT WITH HIS FIST ACROSS ED'S FACE SENDING HIM SPRAWLING..... HE FOLLOWS HIM TO THE FLOOR AND GRABS FOR HIS NECK AS IF TO STRANGLE HIM.....AS THEY STRUGGLE, HE IS SAYING] I told you to shut up.....now shut up or I'll kill you.....I swear to God that I'll kill you......

ED: [IS SCREAMING UNDER CHICO' WEIGHT.....THE CRIES BRING THE OTHERS IN WITH USUAL] What's going on....what's happening.....? [THEY PULL CHICO OFF.... SEPARATING THE TWO MEN]

SGT: What the hell's going on here?

ED: [HOLDING HIS THROAT AND STAYING AWAY FROM CHICO, WHO IS CRYING IN VIC'S ARMS]..... He's crazy...he's fucking crazy....he tried to kill me.....

[SLOW CURTAIN]

END OF PLAY

JACOB

    Jacob's story illuminates the fact that, despite a life of contact, we often lack an appreciation or understanding of the tribulations and motivations that shaped our parents. That knowledge can, sometimes, prove devastating. It also can be the source of great pride and even redirection. The following play is fictionalized, yet based upon true incidents.

JACOB

A ONE ACT PLAY BY JERRY "JOSH" KONSKER

CAST OF CHARACTERS

SARAH... Age 84 Alert, pleasant looking and well groomed. Dressed in black.

ALICIA... Age 59 Bright, attractive middle aged woman. Sarah's daughter also dressed in black although tailored in a masculine style.

STEVEN... Age 61 Tall and strong looking middle aged man. Sarah's son, dressed in a black suit.

JACOB... Age 22 Husband of Sarah and father of Alicia and Steven. When first introduced he's tall and a handsome young man dressed in casual college clothes. Later in the play he's middle aged, but still tall and solid in appearance.

[SETTING]:

[SPLIT THE STAGE BY MEANS OF LIGHT SHADINGS...

ONE THIRD RIGHT, TWO THIRDS LEFT...

7 - ONE ACT PLAYS

STAGE LEFT IS A NICE SIZE KITCHEN IN THE HOME OF JACOB AND SARAH POLANSKY. THE KITCHEN TABLE WITH A TABLECLOTH, FOUR CHAIRS POSITIONED AROUND IT WITH SOME SERVING PIECES ON TOP.

STAGE RIGHT IS A WALL WITH A SERVING CREDENZA THAT CAN HOLD MORE CUPS, COOKIES, ETC. ON STAGE RIGHT THERE'S A FLAT IN PLACE TO CREATE A SECOND DOOR THAT CAN EXIT ACTORS TO OTHER ROOMS IN THE HOUSE. THE UPSTAGE EXIT IS TO THE FRONT DOOR, REAR WALL SHOWS A REFRIGERATOR, SINK, AND STOVE. THERE ARE SOME EMPTY CHAIRS UPSTAGE.

STAGE RIGHT IS PRESET FOR SCENE TWO. ONE SIX FOOT TABLE SET VERTICALLY WITH TWO CHAIRS ON EITHER SIDE......THIS IS A COLLEGE CAFETERIA.

THE PLAY OPENS WITH LIGHTS DOWN RIGHT.... UP LEFT. THE FAMILY HAS JUST RETURNED FROM A FUNERAL. SARAH AND ALICIA ARE SEATED AT THE TABLE... STEVEN ENTERS FROM UP-CENTER]

SARAH: Are they all gone?

STEVEN: Right down to aunt Golda......she said she'd be back tonight......she really meant in a few hours......and then everyday.......as long as you need her.......

ALICIA: A lot of people said that they'll return tonight.....and then there's all our friends who were working and couldn't get to the funeral.

STEVEN: Don't forget our kids and the grandchildren........

ALICIA: The dining room is absolutely overflowing with more food...deli....chicken....lox and bagels.......you would not believe how much cake and candy.....the only other time I've seen so much cake is in a bakery......

STEVEN: What should we do with it Mom?

SARAH: Leave it dear......my sister had a girl here while we were away.....and another young woman should be here any time now.....she'll know how to straighten everything out and prepare it for later........Alicia....I want you to watch your Aunt Golda...... she's not as strong as she thinks she is.....and you two haven't eaten anything since breakfast......you must be hungry......

ALICIA: We've been nibbling with everyone else......I'll make some fresh coffee......it'll be good for all of us.......

SARAH: If I know your aunt, the coffee is already made.......just add a little milk for me............

ALICIA: All right.....I'll get it.....Stevie?.....black, no sugar?

[HE NOD, SHE EXITS TO OTHER ROOM]

STEVEN: **[HOVERING]**..How are you doing mom?.....this day has to be exhausting for you.....and it's not over yet.......

7 - ONE ACT PLAYS

SARAH: I'm okay dear.......you can stop worrying about my every move......dad's death was not a surprise......he's been ill a long time..........

STEVEN: I know, but -------------

ALICIA: [RETURNING WITH TRAY] Coffee everyone..... and I found an open box of butter cookies.....

[SHE PUTS THE TRAY ON THE TABLE.....GIVES SARAH A CUP AND SAUCER....ALICIA AND STEVEN TAKE FOR THEMSELVES]

STEVEN: What I started to say before, is that I had never been to a military funeral before......it was very impressive......the only time I saw so many veterans was on TV....at Arlington, in DC when they were burying some important General......

ALICIA: Do they do that for everyone?

SARAH: I don't really know, dear.

STEVEN: But the things they said about dad.....I didn't know that he was a war hero?......

ALICIA: He never said anything to us.......

SARAH: He didn't like to talk about it......

STEVEN: But mom,.....two Purple Hearts, a Bronze Star,... and a Distinguished Service Cross...that's just under a Medal of Honor..........he didn't win that as a company clerk.....

SARAH: I knew he enlisted in 1943 when he turned eighteen... and he was a lieutenant when he got out ......it was 1946 and he was already twenty one years old.....

ALICIA: A first lieutenant mom.......not just a lieutenant.....

STEVEN: They said he served in Patten's Third Army....they provided an Honor Guard...and I don't know how many of a gun salute...

ALICIA: And they gave you the flag........it was beautiful.....if funerals can be beautiful......

STEVEN: And you didn't know about all the things he did?

SARAH: **[BECOMING UNCOMFORTABLE WITH THE CONVERSATION]**......I told you......your father didn't like to talk about it.....

ALICIA: Nothing?..........nothing at all?

SARAH: All I remember is,.... he said when they made him a lieutenant, they transferred him to another company, so he was not to boss his buddies

STEVEN: Mom,....if he didn't go to officer's school,....that means he was, what they call, "a battlefield commission"......you got to be pretty good to get that.......and he was still a kid......maybe twenty.......

SARAH: I guess so......let's change the subject!

STEVEN: We'll change it for now......but if Ali is with me....... we're going to find out all about Dad's war record......what he

7 - ONE ACT PLAYS

did....and why he won all those medals......he's got grandchildren and great-grandchildren.......they should know all about him....

SARAH: Do what you want.....I don't want to know..... [GETTING UPSET] your father was never a soldier with me.......and I refuse to believe that that sweet gentle man could have done those things they said.......

STEVEN: Okay....okay....we'll change the subject...

SARAH: That's better.....but I'll tell you this....once, when we first started dating....I casually asked dad what he did in the war... he stiffened up like I never saw before......then he said that he would rather not talk about it......I could see how upset he was......I never asked him again.......

[LIGHTS DIM ON STAGE LEFT AND COME UP SLOWLY ON STAGE RIGHT...SARAH TAKES OFF HER JACKET, WHICH IS BLACK AND PUTS ON A LIGHTER COLORED ONE....THE AUDIENCE CAN SEE THIS.....SHE CROSSES TO STAGE RIGHT AND SITS AT THE TABLE....PICKS UP A BOOK THAT SHOULD ALREADY BE THERE....JACOB, A TWENTY TWO YEAR OLD COLLEGE STUDENT, CARRYING BOOKS, ENTERS, GOES TO THE TABLE]

JACOB: Excuse me.....but is this seat taken?

SARAH: No, but there must be forty others around that are more private.

JACOB: Perhaps so......but none with better scenery......

SARAH: Wow, that is some line......you're flirting with me......

JACOB: Oh no,.....I never flirt......that would be a waste of time.... and, honestly, I haven't got lot of time to waste......

SARAH: That's an even better line....

JACOB: Not really........the dictionary calls flirting superficial or trifling....that's not me......and, to be truthful, I've been wanting to meet you for weeks......but I haven't been able to find a friend in common.......you're very private........Oh yes, **[HE STICKS OUT HIS HAND]** ....I'm Jacob....Jack, if you prefer......may I sit?

SARAH: **[RELUCTANTLY RESPONDING]**...Please...sit..... you win this round.... **[TAKES HIS HAND]**...I'm Sarah......and I prefer Jacob....it has more character.....

JACOB: Does that mean there's to be more rounds?

SARAH: You know, you're a little kooky......but I've noticed you wandering about also......I suspect that more rounds are quite possible....

[LIGHTS DIM RIGHT AND COME UP LEFT.....JACOB EXITS......SARAH

SWITCHES JACKETS AGAIN AND RETURNS TO THE KITCHEN TABLE]

[AS LIGHTS RETURN]

STEVEN: That was some line, mom,.....I don't know why dad didn't pass it to me?

7 - ONE ACT PLAYS

ALICIA: You would have dropped it........

SARAH: It wasn't a line........if nothing else, your father was never devious.......

ALICIA: Devious or not.....it obviously worked.....

SARAH: Well, he was persistent......what he saw in me, I don't know.....

ALICIA: Maybe you don't....but we do.....

SARAH: [CONTINUING]..It wasn't that he was romantic....... but he was warm and caring.......remember, your paternal grandparents were a warm family too.....he got it from them.....

ALICIA: What about when he met your father?......grandpa was tough......

SARAH: Only on the outside......my father was very proud of Jacob's having been in the war, and an officer.......your dad wrapped him right around his little finger......my mother as well....

STEVEN: Sounds like a love story to me......

SARAH: It was.......I loved your father from when I first met him........but protocol made me hide it for a while.....

ALICIA: How long, mom?

SARAH: I guess until the day he proposed........he had everything figured out.....it was at a picnic........that was a standard Sunday for us........so we could be together and separately, and at the same time to study......**[DOORBELL RINGS]**...well, children......

someday, I'll tell you that story too........Steven, get the door......it's probably the waitress..........

[LIGHTS DIM LEFT....COME UP RIGHT......PULL AWAY THE LONG TABLE AND REPLACE IT WITH A SMALL ONE......A PICNIC BASKET ON THE TABLE....TWO CHAIRS....JACOB APPEARS....HE SHOULD CHANGE HIS SHIRT......SARAH AGAIN MOVES FROM LEFT TO RIGHT......HAVE A FANCY SHAWL AT HER CHAIR THAT SHE COULD SLIP OVER HER SHOULDERS]

SARAH: [SEATED]..Jacob, sit down and relax......you're so fidgety today....

JACOB: Well,....this is an important date......

SARAH: What can be that important?.......it's only a picnic so we can be together.........

JACOB: It's an important picnic......

SARAH: I thought our important dates were movies and pizza?....sometimes, even......miniature golf ......

JACOB: But, that's not the point!....

SARAH: [TEASING HIM]...What's the point?....I like the movies.....and pizza.......and even miniature golf......that's why I keep dating you.......for the so very exciting dates.....

JACOB: You know.....you're too much!

7 - ONE ACT PLAYS

SARAH: Too much?.....I thought I wasn't enough ......now, stop being silly and tell me what's on your mind.....

JACOB: Well, based on the two year degree that I already have,....I was offered a job with the Port Authority.....

SARAH: **[EXCITED]**. Jacob......that's wonderful......but what about the next year of school.....and the second degree?

JACOB: That's just it......I go to work......study nights......it may take two additional years......but they'll pay my tuition ....and books

SARAH: I don't know what to say......

JACOB: I'm coming to that....It means that now I'll have more than two cents in my pocket......the salary's forty two hundred a year......plus fringe benefits......that's a lot of money to start...

SARAH: **[STILL INCREDULOUS]** ....It sounds wonderful Jacob......it's what you've wanted......what you've worked so hard for...

JACOB: **[HE SQUEEZES OUT THESE WORDS]**...There's something that I've wanted...even more than the degree...I wanted sometimes to be able to buy you an ice cream cone after the pizza and **[THESE WORDS HE BLURTS OUT]**....I've wanted you to spend the rest of your life with me......**[SARAH SAYS NOTHING......HE WAITS...THEN NERVOUSLY]**..... What do you think?......what do you say?

SARAH: **[SMILING]**...I think I know why I learned to like pizza......and miniature golf......

JACOB: Listen,. I had four hundred dollars left from my army money and I'm going to start drawing salary now **[HE REACHES INTO HIS POCKET AND PULLS OUT A RING CASE]** And I hope you'll like it ....**[PUTS THE RING ON HER FINGER]**

SARAH Jacob....I will love it......and I loved it, even before I saw it...because I love you and **[WITH CLARITY]**...of course I will, and spend the rest of my life with you.....

[THEY CLUMSILY REACH ACROSS THE TABLE TO KISS AS THE LIGHTS FADE FOR PASSAGE OF TIME.....LIGHT UP ON STAGE LEFT....SARAH RETURNS TO KITCHEN]

[LEFT LIGHTS UP FINDS SARAH SEATED AT THE TABLE LEANING BACK...STEVEN IS STANDING..... ALICIA ENTERS FROM UPSTAGE....THEY ARE ALL A BIT DISHEVELED]

ALICIA: Well, they're all gone again......mom, you have to be more than tired...

SARAH: I suppose I am dear......did the waitress leave too?.....I hope you gave her a tip?...**[ALICIA NODS YES]**....well then, you and Steven go home and get some rest........see to your ----------

ALICIA: **[INTERRUPTING]**..No, no, mom.....I'm staying with you tonight.....just so I can get things started in the morning....

SARAH: There's no need --------

ALICIA: I need…..so no argument…..

STEVEN: And I'll be back early too……we'll all get through this together…

SARAH: All right children……I'm really too tired to argue…….

[LIGHTS DIM FOR PASSAGE OF TIME……..ALLOW TIME FOR QUICK COSTUME CHANGES……ALICIA IN A CASUAL BLOUSE…..STEVEN NO TIE……SARAH WILL ENTER IN A BATHROBE……LIGHT UPSTAGE LEFT ONLY…..IT IS THE NEXT MORNING…..ALICIA IS SEATED AT THE TABLE DRINKING COFFEE……STEVEN, ENTERING FROM UPSTAGE, DROPS HIS JACKET ON AN UPSTAGE CHAIR]

STEVEN: Morning Ali……how's she doing?

ALICIA: Still sleeping I guess……..although I heard her moving around during the night……..how'd you sleep?

STEVEN: Hardly at all…..kept thinking about dad…..and how little we might have understood about him……did some research on the internet too…….

ALICIA: What about?

STEVEN: About Patton's Third Army in Europe….in World War II……dad was a part of it……..I know the division……got to find out more…we'll have to push mom a little harder……she knows more than she's saying……

ALICIA: **[ADMONISHING HIM]**…Not too hard!

STEVEN: It's so bizarre to believe......that that man......that man who loved peace so much......who wouldn't even let me play with guns when I was little......could have done the things they said......

ALICIA: Yet, mom insists she didn't know......

STEVEN: Maybe.....but I can't understand how.....

SARAH: **[ENTERS FROM THE OTHER ROOM.....SHE IS WEARING A BATHROBE]**....Good morning everyone....... coffee ready?

ALICIA: You know it is.......**[GIVING HER A CUP]** what would you like with it?

SARAH: Maybe a little juice and some toast....**[SHE KISSES STEVEN AND SITS AS ALICIA GETS THE JUICE AND PUTS UP THE TOAST]** How did you sleep dear?

STEVEN: Rather unevenly......kept thinking about dad.....and all the things we didn't know....Mom, you've been holding back!

ALICIA: **[RETURNING TO THE TABLE WITH JUICE AND TOAST]**...Lay off Steve........we were quite surprised...... so many people asked us about all that was said at the funeral, we had to plead ignorance

SARAH: I had to do the same....

STEVEN: But there is more than you've told us......we really have to know.....

SARAH: There's little more to tell you......it's not such a great deal......snippets maybe.....as open as your father was, he

7 - ONE ACT PLAYS

was very private about his days in the army......I remember my father questioning how he became an officer.....and dad cut him short........

STEVEN: That's just the point......it's not normal......there must be reasons....

SARAH: STEVEN, please,...this week is hard enough without you driving me crazy......your father was a very good man...leave it at that!

ALICIA: STEVE!!....enough......**[STEVEN LEAVES THE ROOM]**

SARAH: What time did Golda say she was coming over?

ALICIA: Actually, I thought she'd be here by now.....you slept late.....

SARAH: Not exactly.......but I lay awake a long time......I think when your aunt comes, I want to spend some time with her alone.....

ALICIA: All right......whatever you want......I want to call the grandchildren anyway........mom, why don't you go into the living room......relax in a soft chair....maybe you'll doze off until Golda arrives......

SARAH: Okay, but I'm bringing my coffee with me....**[SHE RISES....TAKES THE CUP AND LEAVES THE ROOM]**

ALICIA: **[CALLING AFTER HER]**...I'm sure the girl left some food open on the table......eat something....anything.....

STEVEN: [**RE-ENTERS**]....I think mom fell asleep as soon as she sat down...Ali, I just can't ignore this.......I called dad's VFW Hall......some of the men who were at the funeral, they were there.......they know more about dad than we or mom do.....a few are dropping in this afternoon......I promised food and something to drink......we can talk to them quietly then.....

ALICIA: But really quietly, you can be very obnoxious when you get a bug up your ass, we don't want mom to realize what you're doing

STEVEN: We'll be discreet.......discreet is my middle name..... you've always known that.....

ALICIA: Of course I do........and when we were teenagers, if I told you that I liked a certain boy........he knew it the next day......I'm still trying to get even with you for that........Mr. Discreet.....

STEVEN: Anyway, between the internet and his friends, maybe we'll get a complete story......it's still so hard to believe.....the man who would go to classical music concerts and the ballet, a God damned war hero.......

ALICIA: You mean ballet and hero can't go together?

STEVEN: Of course they can......they obviously did.....everything just doesn't seem to fit......

ALICIA: It doesn't have to fit......

STEVEN: You're right......I know that......but my gut tells me that mom knows a lot more than she's admitting.....dad wasn't always a quiet man, or at all docile....I remember him threatening to flatten some loudmouth at a little league game.....the guy took one look at dad's eyes and backed down.....dad was a lot tougher than he appeared.......

ALICIA: And I remember him waving at me at High School football games...he didn't care about the game......he just watched me jumping up and down waving pom-poms......I wasn't even very good at it......yeah, he was real tough.

STEVEN: Although he never talked about the war or the fighting, he did tell us about the Holocaust.............and the Nazi death camps.....the things he saw when they liberated those camps......

ALICIA: And that a whole portion of his mother's family, from Rodom in Poland, where his mother's family were all wiped out by the Nazis.

STEVEN: He'd get upset at genocide anywhere......Bosnia, Serbia......the Sudan or Uganda......I recall once....him getting angry throwing the Times Sunday paper on the floor screaming, "Won't these people ever learn?......killing, killing, killing....how can we keep ignoring it?"

ALICIA: I guess we never put two and two together.....he was a much more complicated man than we ever gave him credit for......

[DOOR BELL RINGS]

ALICIA: That would be Golda now......I'll get her.......then I'll make sure we're ready for the next onslaught of guests......

STEVEN: Isn't the waitress coming back to do that?

ALICIA: Yes, but I can't sit still.......besides, some of that Danish is delicious.....and I have a lot of calls to make.......

STEVEN: Me too.......then I want to get back on the internet.....

[LIGHTS FADE FOR PASSAGE OF TIME........ALLOW FOR ALICIA TO HAVE A MINOR COSTUME CHANGE....BLOUSE IS ENOUGH AND STEVEN A SHIRT.....WHEN SCENE OPENS....ALICIA IS ALONE PUTTING OUT CUPS AND SAUCERS......STEVEN ENTERS AND PUTS HIS JACKET DOWN........AS LIGHTS COME UP LEFT]

ALICIA: Two more days......I didn't realize how many people we know.....

STEVEN: And who care for us.....and mom.....and especially dad.....yesterday, when the men from the VFW came over....remember, you met Jimmy Riley?....

ALICIA: Yes, and they all sincerely seemed to like dad.....

STEVEN: I spent a lot of time with them......especially Riley......he said that dad was the most respected member of the post....even though he wasn't too active, but Riley......he served as a non-com in B Company when dad was a lieutenant......not only that.....he was with dad when he won the DSC......

ALICIA: Really?!

STEVEN: Let me start at the beginning.......I have to condense two hours of listening into a few minutes.......here's what Riley told me...he didn't know dad until he became his platoon officer in

7 - ONE ACT PLAYS

Baker Company....... he was obviously a battlefield commissioned office and not a ninety day wonder, he said.......besides, they all heard stories about dad from when he was still a sergeant in Love Company..........

ALICIA: [**NOW INTO IT**]...What about the Purple Hearts?.... and the other stuff?

STEVEN: Riley doesn't know about the first Purple Heart or the Bronze Star .....except what they said at the funeral...he wouldn't even know about the second Purple Heart or the DSC, except that he was with him......the story is this......Baker company was part of the 359th Regiment.....and that they were the lead company advancing to relieve the forces trapped in the Battle of the Bulge........it was winter......they ran into a series of gun emplacements and machine gun nests across a narrow pass by a river......the whole battalion was stopped.....dad took a whole platoon,....of about twenty volunteers........Jimmy included....he said that they were all a bunch of crazy young kids......who'd been fighting the Germans for, what seemed forever,....since Normandy.......to quote him..." It was so cold, they were freezing their nuts off'"...

ALICIA: Stop digressing and stay with the story, please.....

STEVEN: Anyway, they found a place to cross the river about two miles downstream...they ran into some enemy and took fire... dad and two others got hit...the bullet that hit him passed through his arm, so the medic patched him up.....somehow, they got behind the German small artillery position and the machine guns...... dad had spread the unit......three to a target and they did the job....even though they were exposed for twenty or so yards.......it was the element of surprise that worked for them.......dad led the charge.........five men got killed and six more wounded......but they got it done.....when dad got back from the hospital a week later, the battalion CO promoted him to First Lieutenant and made him the company exec officer.....they put him in for the Medal of Honor, but he got the DSC....the rest of them got Bronze Stars... the ones who died, got Silver Stars

ALICIA Wow, that's some story......you know.....when you think about it....they really were kids....twenty....twenty one our kids, at age twenty had to be reminded to brush their teeth......

STEVEN: Jimmy said there was one more story we should know about...about a month before the war ended, the company freed a concentration camp near Prague......he said he never saw anything else like it.......the people were walking dead.....starving......the German SS had run away.........he said that dad went crazy...... even though he was in charge, he wanted to kill every German he could find.......it was terrible......dad did whatever he could to help these people.......he was the only one who could speak their Jewish language.......we gave them all our food.... he sent two big trucks back to get more food, clothes and blankets.......he was a one man dynamo.......

ALICIA: My God, no wonder dad told us about the holocaust..... and why he always got so mad at the idea of ethnic cleansing....

STEVEN: I went on the internet last night........the camp was called the Flossenberg Concentration Camp.......there were about fifteen hundred still alive when freed......almost all Polish......

ALICIA: We better eat something......I have to digest this before mom comes in.....

7 - ONE ACT PLAYS

STEVEN: You stayed here again last night?

ALICIA: I had to....it's too soon to leave her alone......

STEVEN: Do you think she might stay with one of us for awhile?

ALICIA: I broached the idea......it got kind of a cold reception.....we'll have to see.....

SARAH: **[ENTERING ...A LITTLE BRIGHTER]**..Good morning children... I can smell the coffee......

ALICIA: You slept better?

SARAH: Yes dear,.....but it will take time learning to be alone.....

STEVEN: You'll never be alone!

SARAH: I know, I have you guys... and all the children.......I'll get used to the circumstance..............and physically, I'm much stronger than you think.....

STEVEN: Mom, I have to be honest with you.......we've been learning about dad's war record and some of the things he did.....

SARAH: I don't care to know.........dears, listen to me.....I'm fully aware that you father experienced unmentionable things while in the service.........he chose not to talk about them and I respected that......

ALICIA: But there had to be times when he was exposed?

SARAH: There were,.......but they were rare.......once, when we were still very young......he stopped a rowdy drunk at my girlfriend's wedding……..dad just grabbed him and twisted his arm around his back……..it was so quick, I didn't even see him do it……

STEVEN: I don't know if they taught Judo in World War II……. he must've learned it elsewhere…..maybe as a kid……

SARAH: Also, we never went to war movies…….or any of those violent terrible films……you know, the garbage that's always being advertised……..but one war movie he wanted to see……Private Ryan…….he was curious because we heard so much about it….my God……those first twenty minutes……..he gripped the arm rests so tight, I could see his knuckles….white…..even in the dark……. then he got up and left the movie……..later, he said to me that everyone should be forced to see those minutes…maybe, then, they wouldn't be so anxious to make wars……

STEVEN: You know, dad was in the Normandy invasion, but landed on the third day…..even then he went through a helluva lot…it had to leave a helluva mark on him…..

SARAH: I'm sure it did…….perhaps, that is why he was such a peaceful man……..and I loved him for that……and I loved your father very much…….except….I am still mad at him…..

ALICIA: Mad?....what on earth for?

SARAH: He wanted Steven to go to Vietnam……..it was 1969……. many young men were going to Canada….it was a bad war….

ALICIA: I'm sure he didn't want Steve to ------

SARAH: Yes!....yes he did......I said that Steven should go to Canada if he was called.......your father objected......we fought about it for a long time........

[LIGHTS FADE LEFT AND COME UP ON STAGE RIGHT.....THROW A COVER ON THE TABLE...... JACOB IS PRESENT......A MORE MATURE MAN...... SARAH IS YOUNGER TOO]

JACOB: [**STANDING**]...If they leave this country, they shouldn't come back.....they shouldn't even be allowed back..... you don't want be a citizen......don't live here.....this country's too good for you........and that goes for my son too......

SARAH: You want him to die in Vietnam?

JACOB: I don't want anyone to die in Vietnam......we don't belong in Vietnam........but running away won't get us out of Vietnam... and running away won't help him or America.......running away will haunt him......

SARAH: You make arguments like a politician.....not a father......

JACOB: You like this country?......you eat good in this country?... your grandfather came from Poland to this country.......else you would have died in the camps that we saw....

SARAH: That's an old argument....

JACOB: That should never be an old argument......everywhere else Jews die........here you go anywhere......to school.....to live in your own house......to get fat......

SARAH: So what?

JACOB: So you defend this country or you lose it......

SARAH: There are plenty of people who want to be heroes...... to fight in a war.....

JACOB: You don't know what you're talking about!......

SARAH: And the judges and the politicians.......their kids don't go....or else they get jobs that don't get them killed.......

JACOB: Some do....some don't.....

SARAH: So, why can't we do like them........protect our son...... avoid the war.......

JACOB: Not by going to Canada......a pox on all those who go......

SARAH: They'll all come back after the war......

JACOB: I don't want them back......they don't deserve this country....they gave up America......let them go live in Poland or on a Shtetl or a Gulag in Russia......they should live in such places .....those people.......

SARAH: There are no more Shtetls or Gulags........

JACOB: I know......because all the people died in the death camps and the Gulags.......if these kids could see those camps.......they'd maybe realize how important this country is......

7 - ONE ACT PLAYS

[LIGHTS FADE OUT RIGHT AND COME UP LEFT........SARAH RETURNS TO THE KITCHEN....... THE CONVERSATION RESUMES]

SARAH: [**TO ALICIA AND STEVEN**]...And that was only one of the arguments I had with your father........I think we had one a week for a year or more.....

ALICIA: Did you ever try to find out why he felt that way?

SARAH: He felt that way because he's a man and... men don't know a mother's love, men are afraid to show fear, they need be macho.

STEVEN: Mom, I don't think that you can dismiss dad's feelings that way...that simply.....he was always a very positive person..... he taught us to be positive......I'm sure he didn't want me to die in Vietnam.... besides, the decision would be mine.....

ALICIA: He taught us to take on a myriad of challenges......to push ourselves to bigger and better things..... not to be afraid of failure.......it's often the best teacher.....

SARAH: And he taught you not to be afraid to die?

STEVEN: That was never an issue......besides, I had a very high draft number....

SARAH: Well, it was an issue with me........and I can't forget.... and I won't forgive......now, let's stop the talk......people should be here very soon....

ALICIA: Okay,....I'll get the coffee.......

[ALL LIGHTS FADE FOR PASSAGE OF TIME… ALLOW FOR MINOR COSTUME CHANGES…..WHEN STAGE LEFT ONLY COMES UP…ALICIA IS IN THE KITCHEN AS STEVEN ARRIVES]

STEVEN: [**PUTTING DOWN HIS JACKET**]. Coffee smells good…..any cake or cookies left?

ALICIA: I'm sure there's some……it's a good thing this is the last day of shiva……the guests eat like barracuda……sit down……I'll get some for you….[**ALICIA LEAVES THE ROOM…..STEVEN SITS …..ALICIA RETURNS WITH GOODIES**]…You're going to gain ten pounds this week…..

STEVEN: Only five…….I just eat half of each Danish…….mom up yet?

ALICIA: I heard her moving around and you're pushing her too much.

STEVEN: Any positive response to her staying with one of us?

ALICIA: Negative…..very negative…..but one of her friends invited her to stay in Florida with her for a while……that, she's considering…

STEVEN: She prefers a friend to us? We'll have to take care of dad's things next week without her

ALICIA: Yes,….but don't push mom ………

STEVEN: Ali,….you know my friend Phyllis……she was here yesterday and we had a long talk………she's a family psychologist, with a million years of experience.......I told her about mom and dad and Vietnam........she had answers for us........it seems that this reaction on dad's part is not that uncommon.....

SARAH: [**ENTERING...GOOD NATUREDLY**]...Are you two busy planning the rest of my life?

ALICIA: Only the morning coffee......

SARAH: Good.......well, all the visitors leave today........I want to make a careful list of all the things I have to do......people to notify....bills to pay........your father's things.......maybe to the wounded veterans.......

STEVEN: Mom,....we'll take care of all that......

SARAH: No....no....I'm not senile yet......and I'm not helpless...... you can assist in some things........but this is part of my life and a part of my marriage.....

ALICIA: Mom, I know you don't want to talk about it, but Steve and I are almost haunted about our father........we must understand him better........just give us a chance........

SARAH: [**TIGHTENING**] All right.....but keep it simple.....

STEVEN: Mom, I spent a good deal of time with a close friend of mine....a psychologist........and a woman.....I asked her about dad and Vietnam......she explained a great deal.......about dad and all veteran soldiers......especially those who were involved in combat......and we know now that dad did........the post war stress syndromes that everyone talks about now are not new.....all soldiers who were in combat have it........some worse than others....

only in dad's time they were told to put it aside and get on with their lives……..they did……..most of them…but they never were able to fully put it aside………dad was no different…..

SARAH: So….this you didn't have to tell me……..this I knew…….. and this I saw in your father……..but he handled it himself……his own way….

STEVEN: That's just it….his own way…..and when it came to Vietnam he had to deal with it his own way………

SARAH: By letting you go away to die………or to lose a leg…or something?

ALICIA: Mother!

STEVEN: It's okay Ali……..mom, this is what my friend explained to me……almost all soldiers, who have been exposed to death….. and many in very horrible ways…….develop an unconscious and binding sense of protectiveness for their country and their people… they have seen men…..and women too……die for that country…… and now, in their minds, no one has the right to walk away from the responsibility of their citizenship………and then to expect to get it back…….

ALICIA: You've heard the term…. "Love it or leave it".

STEVEN: Mom…..how many times did we have dad remind us of how lucky we are to be here…….born here…..to go to school here…..he certainly didn't want me to die in Vietnam…….he probably didn't even consciously understand his motivations…… but he couldn't let me desert this country……..being a deserter is worse than being a coward………

SARAH So....now you've told me......and now I've heard you... But, I wasn't a Soldier....I was a mother......so, I don't accept why.....I don't accept reasons.......I only accept my son's life......so I still don't forget....I can't quite forgive him.....I still love him my whole life, just as I did that first day......but that doesn't stop me from being mad at him that one time.

[LIGHTS DOWN...END OF PLAY]

A MOVEABLE LIGHT

Written by: JERRY "JOSH" KONSKER

**This play is based upon a true story of my grandparents shortly before World War I*

CAST OF CHARACTERS:

SAM [SHMUEL]: LATE 30's......SHORT BUT VERY SOLIDLY BUILT MAN WHOM OBVIOUSLY WORKS WITH HIS HANDS....VERY SELF CONFIDENT AND IS VIEWED AS A MAN WITH DIRECTION]

BETSY [BEENA]: MIDDLE 30's......BRIGHT RED HAIR......A SMALL BUT ATTRACTIVE WOMAN...... VERY NEAT......SHE HAS WORKED HARD RAISING A FAMILY OF FOUR CHILDREN...HER DRESS IS SIMPLE BUT WELL FITTED AND NEAT]

[THE SETTING:

A MEDIUM LARGE LIVING ROOM OF A BRONX, NEW YORK TENEMENT APARTMENT......A SINGLE LIGHT BULB HANGS FROM THE CEILING... THE FURNITURE IS SOLID WOOD BUT INEXPENSIVE......A COUCH AND TWO CHAIRS...... AN END TABLE AND A COFFEE TABLE......AN ASH

TRAY AND TWO COFFEE CUPS.....NO SAUCERS..... EVERYTHING APPEARS SCRUPULOUSLY CLEAN AND NEAT.......]

[AT OPEN CURTAIN....SAM IS SEATED IN A CHAIR DOWN RIGHT....THE END TABLE NEXT TO THE CHAIR WITH A DICTIONARY ON IT.. HE IS READING A NEWSPAPER....STOPS...PICKS UP THE BOOK ...LOOKS IN AND CLOSES IT......BEENA ENTERS AND SITS OPPOSITE HIM....SHE SIMPLY WATCHES HIM FOR A FEW MOMENTS AND SAYS NOTHING]

SAM: [LOOKING UP]..Oy,.....this American language is very hard......it can take a whole day to read a newspaper......

BEENA: Sam,.......I'm not happy........

SAM: Who's happy?

BEENA: I don't know who's happy........but I know I'm not happy......here!

SAM: You want happy?.......go to the Yiddish theatre......the comedians will make you laugh......

BEENA: Don't make fun on me......I'm not a fool.......this life is not better than what we had in Lodz........for this we had to be separate for three years? to uproot our family?.....did I have to leave my mother and my father?......Sam, look at me......do you want me to go on......are you going to look at my face and talk to me about what is real?........

7 - ONE ACT PLAYS

SAM: What are you talking?......real is food on the table for the supper.....and for the whole family......that's happy....that's real..

BEENA: Goyisha food........

SAM: It's kosher.......you bought it yourself........

BEENA: But not our kind of kosher......

SAM: So, what's our kind?.....

BEENA: Polish.....like in the old country.......

SAM: Danken Gott.......we're not in the old country.......

BEENA: And I don't have enough dishes to separate the milchic from the fleishic......

SAM: It'll take a little longer.......you'll see......we'll have those things....

BEENA: [SHE STARES AT SAM AND SAYS NOTHING..... THEN] There's too much that's not good here......

SAM: Still, the food?......the food is so different?.....the food is better... now we don't live on cabbage and potatoes......now you have some vegetables and fruits with colors on them.......

BEENA: This is not what I'm talking about.......

SAM: So,...what are you talking about?

BEENA: You're not the man I married......you've changed too much.!....

SAM: You know….you're crazy…….almost twenty years we're married… I worked all the time……I was forced in the army two years…..and I'm in America three years……..you want I should be the same man?

BEENA: I'm the same woman!!.....

SAM: Raising the children when I'm in the army?...and three years without me before I could bring you and the little ones here?..... and you think you're the same woman?

BEENA: Inside….inside I'm the same woman…..the happy girl you married.. I can live with hardships……but inside……inside I want to be the happy person you married……

SAM: And I want the beautiful, happy girl I married……now …..we're here in America…….you can throw away the sheitel…… let that beautiful red hair flow freely…….everyone should see the lovely lady that is my wife…….

BEENA: Don't start with the red hair Shmuel……we're talking serious…..

SAM: [ROMANTICALLY] I remember so well…….for three years I played with that hair……twisted it soft as I looked in your eyes……..

BEENA: [BECAUSE HE'S NOT TAKING HER SERIOUSLY] And it could be three years before I let you touch it again…….you would have me grow out my hair?……let my red hair flow in the wind?….the couvres, the whores have hair blowing in the wind……is this what you want?

7 - ONE ACT PLAYS

SAM: Why must it be a bad thing?.........am I only to took at my wife when she's not hiding behind a sheitel and a shawl.......Only I should see her?......how beautiful she is.......I should be such a miser not to share her with the world?

BEENA: Who are you sharing me with?......the pushcart peddlers?....the poor people in the street?......your cronies should see what a prize you got?

SAM: [SOFTLY] My mother,...aliva sholom,......should only see what a prize I got.......

BEENA: [STRNGLY] Shmuel,........it's time now to talk......not to play with hair and not to make fairy tales........are we now Jewish or Yankee Goyim?.....

SAM: It's not like Rodm......or Lodz....or even Warsaw.....it's different Jewish........I don't walk around with my tsisis hanging out of my pants.......does that mean they put the tip back on my schmeckle? I am who I am........but I must also change with the time and the place where we live......

BEENA: It's a goyisha world here.....when I walk around....go two blocks from the apartment......I see Christmas trees all over...... and the people.....they don't look like us.....

SAM: And in Poland they look like us?...... blond hair and blue eyes?.......only in the shtettles did everyone look like us......and they looked like us till the Cossacks and the drunks came.....then they looked bloody and dead......

BEENA: There were no Cossacks in Lodz........they're in Russia.....

SAM: In Lodz we had drunks and anti semites......and how long would it be before Poland is part of Russia again?.....did you forget in 1903,.....the pogrom in Kishinev??...the Czar sat by and laughed...

BEENA: But, for a thousand years......in Poland .... in Russia..... no matter who tried to destroy us.......we survived......we didn't lose God....we didn't lose our way of life......here......here the children will forget who they are.......

SAM: No,.....here they will learn who they are.......look on your son Aaron, ... sixteen years old and he goes to school.......he speaks American......he walks with his head in the sky...... in the high school, a gymnasium, and no quotas....... after school, he helps me........he fixes things......he paints walls.......he's not in the army cleaning horses for the damned Cossacks....... you forgot why we came here?.......so that he and little Hershel should never go in the army like I did.......you forget when I came home?...what I told you?......in the Russian army you fight and you die for who?....for the Czar?...... now I spit on the Czar.....I can do that here......in this country......not there......you forget Beena,? Two years I was away.....when the war was over, they said, "Jew, go home"........ no money,...no food.....nothing......two years cleaning the Czar's horses in Manchuria......."Jew, go home"......they sent Jews to fight the Japanese cannons......sticks they gave us.... not rifles...... sticks against cannons......"Jew, go home".......I don't forget...... it was near the end...the cannon....horses.... the noise.... then, nothing...... I wake up.... it was dark.....no stars.... no moon......no light......I was in a hut....I was smeared with mud.. I know, "don't make a noise".......I try to get up and I fall......I fall on bodies..... in uniforms like mine......they don't move......they're dead......I'm not sure, even, that I'm alive.......the air is still.... "Mama,!....help me".......she can't help me......what to do?....lay there.....think.......

wait for light.......pray to God?.....you can't pray to God........God don't live in such a place........the morning comes.......you find your way back to your side......you clean yourself.........and the cannons start again.... [WITH GREAT STRENGTH] This I won't let my sons ever see.......no one's sons should ever see......... [THE STRENGTH GONE}.....three months it took me to grt home.......working......begging..... walking........I never told you......I almost didn't come......I almost didn't know how to come home.....

BEENA: [SOFTLY} I don't forget.......I don't forget nothing...... we cried, we laughed and we sang......we rejoiced when you came home.........we were a family again.......the most important thing Jews could be........a family.......and I don't forget..... together we said for you and Aaron to come to America......and now, again we are a family.......Aaron is almost a man........but the little ones...... Sophie is seven, Heshel is six and little Anna is five..... this is a new country.....it frightens me......it's not Jewish.....we will lose our children.....God will punish us......

SAM: [FRUSTRATED] He's punished us enough...... He's punished our people enough......and we don't even know what we did to deserve it........[STRONG] I don't want to hear from God punishing me anymore.......

BEENA: SHA......don't even think that way!......He'll strike you down......

SAM: He tried....... two years He tried........and He missed..... it's time for Him to let me alone......{LOUD} I have too much work to do.

BEENA: [CHANGING THE TONE AND TRYING TO CHANGE THE SUBJECT] Shh......you'll wake the children......

Anna has a cold….where is Aaron?.....he should be studying……..the Talmud…and he don't daven too good…..

SAM: He doesn't have to…….it's not important….

BEENA: What's not important?

SAM: The Hebrew…..the Talmud…..nobody talks Talmud here.

BEENA: Shmendriks don't talk Talmud…..shmendriks don't read Hebrew…. my son is no shaigetz and I won't let him become one…..

SAM: Beena please……you're here only a few months…..you're stuck in this apartment with two sick little girls…..you don't know yet this country……it's not Poland….thank God….and it's not a back street in Lodz……this is a different world…….

BEENA: What kind of a world?

SAM: A world where Jews can do like anybody else……..and be like anybody else…….I can go to Shul…..I don't have to go to Shul… I can work on Shabbos….I don't must work on Shabbos…..

BEENA: You're not supposed to work on Shabbos!.....

SAM: If working on Shabbos……when there was work on Shabbos… meant making more money to get you and the kids here sooner……I worked on Shabbos…..and now…to put food in their mouths, I work on Shabbos……….and Aaron,…sixteen years old…….helps me……always…….

BEENA: And this is the price we have to pay to come to America?.... to stop being Jewish?....

7 - ONE ACT PLAYS

SAM: There's Jewish....and there's Jewish......I don't like my face with hair......I don't need my tszitis hanging out......I'm still a Jew.... I don't hide it.....but I don't walk around with a sign either... this is a different life....

BEENA: Sam, I'm frightened.......I have many questions......I don't know if I know you so much any more......I don't know where I am.... I don't even know who I am.......

SAM: So,....who knows?......what did you think would be?....you walked away from the stench and the darkness of Europe..... then you stepped off the boat into the light from America......it takes time to understand......

BEENA: You keep telling me what we're getting... you should think, better what we're giving up......

SAM: We're giving up drek......do I clean the Czar's horses anymore?.... Aaron won't have to........remember....that's why I left....so he wouldn't become cannon shit for the Czar....the Czar don't live here......

BEENA: This country has armies too......

SAM: Only if you join them.......you don't have to be a soldier........

BEENA: Then I must worry about the kinder!........we need a Yeshiva for Hershell........ our girls must learn to read and write...... if my father taught me....then I must teach them too.....

SAM: [NOW GETTING LIGHTER] Not agreed and agreed......Heshy doesn't need a Yeshiva......he goes to the American school and he'll go to the Cheder.....Cheder is enough....

it won't be his whole life......the girls?.....like all girls in America, they'll go to the school.......they'll read, they'll write, they'll do numbers.... for you,....Heshy gets the Cheder,...the girls get the school....for me,...I don't care any more.......

BEENA: Your dead grandfather is hearing you.......he's crying!

SAM: When I got on the boat to come here, they told me......"You get halfway across the ocean,.....throw away your prayer shawl and your philacteries".........Beena, ...I can see......a man who sits in Shul all day.....in this country... ...he can't feed his family.....

BEENA: Maybe, we should have gone to Palestine with the Zionists?..

SAM: And what?......raise mosquitos?......be sensible woman.....

BEENA: But you don't go to Shul.......hardly at all......

SAM: Wrong!.....not at all.......I should go to Shul with the billygoats three time a day.....I should listen to those idiots mumble five hundred times that God is great.......if God is so great....he knows it already.......he don't need me to keep telling Him......

BEENA: Shmuel,......it's hard to talk to you anymore.......you don't make sense to me enough.......it's so hard to be happy here......to be comfortable......I'm thinking,...maybe we should go back....things have changed there......life is better for the Jews.......

SAM: In Poland?.......in little Russia? is better?.......a little vodka and your Polish friends will come to visit you at night........with sticks and swords and clubs.......

7 - ONE ACT PLAYS

BEENA: You forget when my father and his friends beat them with whips...

SAM: So they wait a little time....and so they forget...and then they come back.......we need the Czar to send his animals again?.......he killed thousands........not just a few.......our families were lucky..... in the big cities we were stronger.....and we could hide.....a little safer.... but, in the villages?........poof!......[CHANGES HIS TONE]..Beena, I don't want to fight with you........I want, we should be partners......there's three young children.....they should grow up to be Americans.......and our grandchildren will be doctors and lawyers....men of letters.......they'll go to any school they want......and will be anything they can ....

BEENA: How do I do this when I'm afraid to walk in the street?

SAM: Very soon you'll walk in the street...... you'll say hello to everyone.......and you'll say in American......"hello".....Polish, you throw in the garbage......Hebrew is for old rabbis......I want you should teach the children to speak Yiddish too......they'll always have Yiddishkeit......they will be, "A light unto the Nations,".............see,......you think I forgot everything our fathers taught us?

BEENA: And it's for me to teach the history to the children?

SAM: Why not?.......you know it better than me........

BEENA: But your family........your grandfathers were the Talmudists.....

SAM: So,....maybe it's time for a woman to be a Talmudist?....to read it and to teach it.........I'm to busy painting and fixing.....you'll be their teacher at home……and you'll take them to the American school……..you'll help them…..

BEENA: And my Aaron?…….is he too old for the school?

SAM: He's a smart boy………handsome……he'll find his way…..

BEENA: First, must finish the school?

SAM: He'll finish…….I promise…..he speaks American already…. hell work too…..he can do what he likes…..what he's able….he won't be like his greatgrandfather pulling, like a horse, his wagon for forty years…….he can make a business…..he can work for somebody else……..no one from the government to tell him he can't……..

BEENA: And if Aaron gets married?

SAM: He's still got pimples on his face…..who's going to marry him?

BEENA: But he's such a handsome boy……

SAM: So, if he gets married, I'll worry then……..or better…..I'll let his wife's father worry….

BEENA: Oy,….my head is all mixed up……it is happening too fast……no other woman in my family learned to read…….only me..my father said he only has a girl…"she will learn to read like the men"…..my cousins, the red heads,…..they're all men…..they can hardly read….they're ignorant…not taught…not studied……..

SAM: But, if they work hard......in this country.....they'll take care of their families.......our children?.....they must be better.....it's your job........

BEENA: And will they lose the light, the knowledge, we Jews are supposed to keep alive.......they could forget they're Jews.........

SAM: They won't forget......you will teach them well......they'll be good Jews here..... learn their history and the light will be in them......in the stupid walled city we called Lodz......the only light we saw was in the Shabbos candles we had as a family......all else was dark........

BEENA: Then we'll still have Shabbos here?........ a family?......or else I want to take the children and go back......Lodz was not as dark Like you say.......

SAM: Don't talk nonsense!

BEENA: [STRONG} Not nonsense......there is much that makes me unhappy in this city.....

SAM: What else is in your silly head now?

BEENA: [SLOWLY} A woman Shmuel.....there was a woman!!!

SAM: There is no woman!....

BEENA: Three years and no woman?........no hanky panky?

SAM: What do you want from me?

BEENA: You changed too much.......you're not the man I married in Poland...this country is too good for you......you like to be a Yankee.......

SAM: So!..........what do you want from me?

BEENA: The truth........for three years you didn't fix toilets and paint all the time........or take Aaron to school........

SAM: I went to the Yiddish theater........I played cards......there's plenty landsman here........and your crazy cousins.......

BEENA: My cousins are good men........don't make them bad.......

SAM: Good?......Harry is good......we paint together......but he drinks a lot........Moishe, the dairyman?........he's a good man..... works hard......found a nice young wife........and Red .....Fiebish?.... he's a goniff........he steals.......he's gonna get caught and wind up in jail.............crazy red headed bastard........that's your cousins........

BEENA: [NOT RELENTING] You still didn't tell me about the woman ....

SAM: No woman!!........women!!!.....there's lots of women here from the old country.......their husbands ran away...... disappeared......they're hungry for a man......they're here to be had.......for almost any body.......there's no love.......there's only animal......I'm an animal too........but now you're here.......I sent for you......for the children.......I'm here.......I didn't go away......I worked......I made money......for you....for the children........and sometimes I drank too much......and sometimes I found myself in someone's bed.....so what?.....I didn't bring them home.....Aaron

7 - ONE ACT PLAYS

don't know.....so, now you're here......and I'm here.....there is no one else here.....or anywhere........

BEENA: [SITTING....SOMEWHAT OVERWHELMED] I don't know.....I don't know........is this the life we should have?....... this is not the Ketubah.........not the vows......this is foreign........ not the Jewish way........it's a foreign way.....a foreign country......

SAM: No........you are dreaming the wrong dream......this is our country now.......this is not foreign......Poland is foreign.......you think men didn't run around in Poland?......they didn't cheat on their wives?........what were you, blind?......you knew what was going on........you didn't want to see it........how many women are still there?.......sitting with their children?......waiting for a letter to bring them here?........and the letter doesn't come........and so they wait........and they'll wait until the Messiah comes.....you didn't wait forever....you came as soon as I had the money......but I'm not a holy man...only in the books you read are holy men, maybe your father shouldn't have taught you to read......you read too many books.......too many fairy tales......where all the women are pure, and all the men keep their pants on......

BEENA: And now you're going to keep your pants on?

SAM: [SOFTLY] Only for you, Beena, only for you do I take them off!!!! [THEY STARE SILENTLY AT EACH OTHER FOR A FEW MOMENTS...AND THEN SAM CONTINUES]......Beena...for us, do this,.... I'll make for you a special promise.......give us, our family,....two years in America..... in these years, I will work hard.......you will learn American ways and raise the children.......Aaron will finish school......he will be a man to make his own decisions.......the time is now summer, it's 1913.........in two years...... the summer 1915..... If you're still unhappy.....not comfortable......we will talk about going back to Poland........or to maybe,...Palestine.....or even, like the English are talking.......Uganda........

[FADE TO BLACK........END OF PLAY]

THE STIFLING

A One Act Play

Written By: Jerry "Josh" Konsker

****The Stifling is a story of a family's addressing the newness and the possible complexities of multi-racial marriage. However, in this instance, it is not the matching of two progressive young people but of the generation first introduced to the racial equality laws of the 1960s. The story has its origin in an incident between two very young people in 1940. The memory has never gone away.*

Cast of Characters: In order of appearance

Carol:	69 years old, attractive, well dressed black woman
Ralph:	72 years old, tall, medium build, nicely dressed white man
Melanie	38 years old, Carol's daughter
Sam	42 years old, Carol's son in law
Sandy	44 years old, Ralph's daughter in law
Stanley	46 years old, Ralph's son
Cheryl	41 years old, Ralph's daughter
Alex	44 years old, Ralph's son in law
James	9 years old, Melanie's son
Webster	6 years old, Melanie's son

SCENE ONE

[THE EXTERIOR OF A COFFEE SHOP ON MADISON AVENUE IN MANHATTAN NEW YORK......NEAR THE METROPOLITAN MUSEUM OF ART.....IN THE LOW EIGHTIES....RALPH AND CAROL ARE SEATED AT A SMALL TABLE HAVING COFFEE AND CONVERSATION]

RALPH It's hard to believe how I feel with you..........sometimes, I'm like a twelve year old back in grade school.....[FLIRTING]... but I have to tell you,.....you're much better looking than the Mrs. Hanrahan that I remember in the fifth grade......

CAROL: Not having met her Ralph, I'm afraid to take that as a compliment....

RALPH: Put it in your book.......a double compliment......as a teacher....and as a looker....

CAROL: A looker?......your choice of words is, sometimes, an education for me.....is that another strange sports term of yours?

RALPH: Nope.......what's wrong with looker?

CAROL: Nothing, I'm sure.....I just never heard the word used that way before......especially for me......[OVERACTING]......I humbly accept your very generous compliment.....

RALPH: You're putting me on.....I don't believe you never heard it that way.....[CHANGING THE SUBJECT]]......you know, I've lived in New York my entire life........and until I met you, I never went to this museum...the Metropolitan Museum of Art.......or any other one in this city......

CAROL: Really?

RALPH: I remember once .....in school......maybe the sixth or seventh grade, we took a bus to the Museum of Natural History..... the one across the park......I always remember the dinosaur and the whale......but that's the only one......oh yes......I once took the kids to the baseball Hall of Fame in Cooperstown......

CAROL: I've been there......my husband was a sports nut......we went to the basketball hall in Springfield also......Isaac was still playing horse with his friends until the day he died......he was good at it too.......but you needn't apologize.....you've had a very busy life, Ralph......working long hours.....raising a family....most of the time you worked two jobs.. you told me so yourself.........

RALPH: I told you so.....yes....but not so you'd feel sorry for me......

CAROL: How the devil could I feel sorry for you?.........you're one of the sweetest and most generous persons that I've ever known..... even though you're a Met fan.....

RALPH: Generous?.......I can't be too generous on a limited retirement income......

CAROL: Generous has many forms.......only a few are related to money.. besides, you make me feel warm......and wanted....and important...

RALPH: The warm part I don't do so good any more either.....

CAROL: And you're a comedian......you make me laugh....

RALPH: All right, I'm a comedian........a few jokes I can tell......

CAROL: C'mon Ralph.......don't play humble.....you know darn well that it's not any jokes......so now.....we just spent four hours in the museum......what did you think?

RALPH: I think you can be a very tricky lady.......first some singles....and then doubles.......and now a home run......

CAROL: An interesting analogy, but I believe I get it.....

RALPH: You should.......you like baseball........first you take me downtown to Soho.......some fancy and not so fancy art galleries.. then the Museum of Modern Art.....and the Neue Museum where you show me Klimt paintings......and now the Metropolitan.....

CAROL: So?

RALPH: The truth?......down in Soho, some of those artists have a high opinion of themselves....and a lot of them make a lot of junk.. I can spot a phony without being a so called "art expert".......a man twists two pieces of metal together, and then he gives it a fancy name and a high price......and the tries to call it a new art form......it's garbage......and that's because he doesn't know how to do anything else........

CAROL: And the doubles?

RALPH: That's different.....it's nice....it's pretty.....I guess it must be good 'cause so many people say it's good.......smart people.... like you......you studied this....you taught this in high school and college...I respect that......but I don't see what you all see......perhaps I'm too dumb ....?

CAROL: Ralph dear,.....you're certainly not dumb.....perhaps....as time goes on, I'll be able to show you how I see it......look, I know a lot of very smart people who, also, don't particularly care for modern art......

RALPH: Why don't some of these new painters paint in the old traditions?

CAROL: Many do......you saw some of them today..you just didn't realize that they were contemporary...

RALPH: I guess but today......today...you hit a home run.....these pictures I could understand.....I could even feel the religious ones that weren't Jewish........and your guy Rembrandt.....of course, I always heard of him.....but today he talked to me......I could hardly believe what beautiful things he made...

CAROL: Someday.......maybe soon......we'll go to Amsterdam and you'll see the painting they call "The Nightwatch".....that'll really blow your mind.....

RALPH: [GETTING SERIOUS]..Carol,.....it's time we talk...important things......you know that I love you.......I never thought that I could love someone this way again.......but I do......and today.....today has been wonderful.....as has so many days in these last six months.....and I know that you like me a little too.....so the question is.....what do we tell the children?.....how do I explain that a beautiful and educated woman, like you, is willing to spend this part of her life with an ordinary guy like me?

CAROL: I have no idea what you define as ordinary......but I do know, that whatever you're thinking, it doesn't apply to you...... you know so much more about life than I do......so many things you've introduced me to......things I never could have learned shut up in the monastery called "academic institutions".....so stop putting yourself down.....we will tell the children the truth.....that we've been almost inseparable since we met......that we are now living together....which I am sure they realize already......but most important.....that we've looked at all the pros and the cons.....that the pros outweigh the cons......and, therefore, we have decided to get married.....

RALPH: So it looks like we're going to start with your two daughters.. only one is here now.....I think girls should be easier than boys...besides, we're having dinner with Melanie and Sam tonight......

[END OF SCENE]

7 - ONE ACT PLAYS

[SCENE 2......LIGHTS UP ON AN ITALIAN STYLE RESTAURANT...CHECKERED TABLE CLOTHS...... CAROL, RALPH, MELANIE, AND SAM ARE COMFORTABLY SEATED SIPPING WINE....]

MELANIE: Mom....what makes you think that this is a surprise to us...gosh, I haven't heard that pleasant lilt in your voice since dad died.... this sounds terrific.......

SAM: Ralph, you and I are bonding already.....we're both Met fans.. we will suffer together.....

RALPH: It gets worse for me......now I'm half a Marlin fan too....I suffer all year round.....and the two of us will commiserate over the Jets and the Giants later....

SAM: Don't forget the Knicks......it's like they haven't won in my lifetime....

MELANIE: Will you two shut up already?....I want to put in first dibs as the matron of honor......

CAROL: If your sister can get home from the Middle East, I'll have both of you next to me.....

MELANIE: I hope you hear from Althie more than I do....even with telephones and texting.....it's every two weeks, if I'm lucky...

CAROL: With me, it's about once a week......but she worries me so much......all those dangerous places....and people.....and they don't respect women there .....

MELANIE: Mom,….you and dad taught her…..she sees herself representing your values…..what you would do…..would you have her do otherwise?……she's one of the few black women who can make their voices heard…..and even more, the voices of black and brown women all over that part of the world…..mom, she's doing good things…..dad would be proud……

CAROL: I am too, dear,…..but that doesn't stop me from being a worried mother…..

SAM: Enough worrying for the moment…..let's get back to the event at hand……..when do you two want to do this wondrous thing?...and let it be known…..Mel and I would love to host it in our house….all the kids and grandkids…..and anyone else you guys would like to invite…..

RALPH: What a nice suggestion…..I think that would be great… and very thoughtful of you both…..but first we want to sit down with Cheryl and Stan, my daughter and son……then we want to put you all together…..to become friends……but I promise you…. we're not stalling…..

SAM: Good…….I'll tell the house to wait…..anyway Ralph, I want you to meet our boys……

RALPH: For that I won't wait…….they play Little League?…… you have real baseball fields on Long Island, don't you?…….you should see the fields in Florida…..with night lights too…..where we lived in the Bronx, you couldn't have a real baseball field…… it was all cement…..maybe a softball field in the schoolyard we had…..my Stanley, he played a lot of basketball…..

MELANIE: Can I ask a question that's sitting in the back of my head?

CAROL: Of course dear......

MELANIE: As I understand it.....mom, you're giving up your rented apartment.....and you're living in Ralph's condo?

RALPH: Sure....

MELANIE: Ralph,.....I assume that most of the people living in your development are Jewish.......will mom be the only black face in a sea of white.?

CAROL: Melly, that's not a fair =====

RALPH: [VERY POSITIVE]...No Carol.......it's a very fair question....and it deserves a very honest answer.....the answer, my dear, is she will not be alone......true, most of the people are Jewish......but we have some black, some brown, and some Hispanic......even some Asians......you do know, I hope, that there are black Jews too.....we're a religion, not a race......but the most important thing is that we're up to our touchas with teachers....... your mother fit's in very easily.....in fact, she already has.......you don't have to worry about her.......everybody wants to be her friend.....you'll see.....she'll be very happy.......you will visit with the kids.......we have plenty of rooms and a big community pool..... besides, the rent is cheap.......trust us.....

CAROL: Melanie....Sam....I can only echo what Sam said....and remember, I've been there for a few months now.......

MELANIE: Okay......we're good....but I had to ask.....

CAROL: Certainly you did.......we considered that a possible problem a while back......it's not an issue......

SAM: All right then.....a toast.....raise your glasses......wine...iced tea.......whatever......to Carol and Ralph.......a new beginning.....

[DIM LIGHTS....END OF SCENE].

7 - ONE ACT PLAYS

SCENE 3

[THE DINING AREA AND FAMILY ROOM OF STANLEY AND SANDY'S HOME......A DINING ROOM TABLE AND CHAIRS.....THREE COMFORTABLE CHAIRS AND A FEW SMALL TABLES.....WHEN LIGHTS COME UP....CAROL AND SANDY ARE SEATED IN CONVERSATION]

SANDY: I really envy you in a way.....my Stanley's a great husband....with me.....with the children.....my family....but he's got a way to go before he attains the charm of his father......but he'll get there....I just have to wait......

CAROL: That's an interesting description, coming from you.....I have felt the charm in Ralph.....but he just jokes about it......refuses to take himself seriously.......

SANDY: He would......but Carol, although we hardly know each other yet.....I do know that it took a very special person to crawl back into Ralph's heart......he's been awfully sad sometimes......

CAROL: Sandy.......you never quite know how lonely you've been, until you stop being lonely......I guess that's what has happened to both of us......and then to add to the euphoria.....sometimes, in your seniority, you have unlimited time......it can be like a child in a candy store with a pocket full of money......

SANDY: And your candy stores are the art museums?.....do you paint too?

CAROL: I've tried........and a few things are nice...but nothing spectacular......that's why I chose to teach art history....as opposed to starving....

SANDY: I'm glad to hear it…..I hate that old bromide that says, "Those that can't do, teach instead."……I've known a lot of doers who can't teach worth a damn……the colleges are full of them…..

CAROL: You're right…..a person can teach technique in painting or in music…..or even forms and method in writing without being artistically proficient……certainly, one can teach appreciation….at least I hope so..

SANDY: You're being modest……

CAROL: I hope that too…..

[RALPH AND STANLEY ENTER…THEY ARE JOVIAL]

STAN: Well everyone,….the champagne is on the ice…..the ice cream is in the freezer……the birthday girl is here……but Sandy, have you heard from Cheryl?

SANDY: She called……they were delayed waiting for a delivery…should be here any time now…

RALPH: Maybe you have some beer in the house?…..Ying Ling?….champagne gives me heartburn…..

STAN: Pop, you bring home a very classy woman…..and you're still asking for beer…..I don't believe you…..

RALPH: Believe me…….Sam Adams, if you don't have Ying Ling….

CAROL: It's okay Stan……it's his false humility……he's really a very upscale gentleman…….but afraid to show it……

7 - ONE ACT PLAYS

STAN: Okay......and we'll have beer at the wedding .....as well as the champagne......

RALPH: And those little hot dogs for the beer.....

SANDY: Don't worry dad,.....we'll all sit down with Melanie and Sam.....the menu will cover all the bases.....including little hot dogs....

CAROL: I am so sure you guys will all like each other....

STAN: If Melanie is anything like you....I may fall in love with her myself.......but don't tell Sandy....

CAROL: Sandy, you don't have to wait....he's just like his father already.....

[CHERYL AND ALEX ENTER.....SHE IS CARRYING A LARGE GIFT WRAPPED BOX......ALEX HUGS RALPH.....SLAPS STAN ON THE BACK...KISSES SANDY ON THE CHEEK....A BIT AWKWARDLY KISSES CAROL ALSO....STAN KISSES CHERYL, WHO, IN TURN, KISSES RALPH, STAN AND CAROL]

CHERYL: [REFERRED TO AS SHERRY] Happy birthday Sandy....welcome to the age of mmmmm....[SHE STOPS AND TAKES CAROL IN BOTH HANDS]....and you, of course, are Carol....it's wonderful to finally meet you......you're all dad talks about.....

CAROL: I'm very happy to be here.....and to meet you all.... if you're only half as good as Ralph tells me you are....you're all destined for sainthood......

ALEX: Enough of the platitudes.....I'm starving for birthday cake...I don't get fed enough at home......

CHERYL: You can't lie.....your belly gives you away....

ALEX: Carol,........have you any idea of how difficult it is to live with a woman who doesn't like Chinese food.....and is ambivalent about ice cream?

CHERYL: I think you're looking in the wrong place for sympathy.....Carol....more important....tell us how you became a docent.....

ALEX: First.....get the cake and open the presents.....

[LIGHTS DIM FOR PASSAGE OF TIME....WHEN LIGHTS COME UP, IT IS A FEW HOURS LATER..... ALL ARE STILL THERE..SOME GIFT BOXES ON THE SIDE TABLE......COFFEE CUPS AND PLATES ON THE COFFEE TABLE.. SANDY IS PUTTING THINGS AWAY......AFTER THE SEATING.....THE ATMOSPHERE REMAINS PLEASANT]

STAN: Dad, I can't believe all the time that you're spending at art museums......your idea of art was a picture of Marilyn Monroe with her skirt being blown up......

RALPH: See what I have to put up with Carol?.....children with no respect.......he thinks that a college education makes him an intellectual....

CHERYL: Don't listen to them Carol......it's a game they've been playing for as long as I can remember.....

7 - ONE ACT PLAYS

RALPH: It's not a game......your brother's a .....what do you call them?.......a pseudo intellectual.....

STAN: Carol.....you're building a monster.....

RALPH: So what?......Carol is teaching me.....she's a great teacher..

CAROL: Not really.....your father's a great learner......seriously, he's like a sponge......everything we see or do sticks right in the folds of his brain.......and he teaches me too......I see things through new eyes.....his eyes......his thoughts.....his life.....

RALPH: And I see through her life......it was no picnic when she was born......the world was even more stupid about black people than it is today.......

CAROL: It was so smart about Jews?

RALPH: Different, you, they thought were inferior......for us..... some thought they were better......but others were afraid that they weren't as good......they were jealous.......it infuriated them.....and others, just simple hate......hate from ignorance.....

ALEX: Unfortunately, that hate is rearing it's ugly head again....

CHERYL: At least we're insulated in America......

RALPH: Not all over......too many meshuganah running around with guns......

ALEX: The NRA has a powerful lobby....

RALPH: They shouldn't even be allowed in the lobby.......

STAN: Dad, let's not get into that one again.......we're all pretty much in agreement......Al, we're planning to meet with Carol's kids....Melanie and Sam......Sam has volunteered their house for the wedding, and =======

CHERYL: [INTERRUPTING]...Wedding?.....what wedding?

STAN: Why, dad and Carol, of course.....

CHERYL: [GETTING VERY VISIBLY UPSET]....What do you mean, "of course".?.....when was this decided?.....nobody said anything about a wedding......

STAN: Cherry.......don't get upset......no one was leaving you out.....we only started talking about it a short while before you and Al got here......

RALPH: We waited......we didn't want to tell you all until we could do it in person.......

CHERYL: But I thought you were just living together?

RALPH: We are......but maybe we're a little old fashioned.....just living together doesn't seem right....

CHERYL: [STRONGLY]..Make it seem right!.......you can't get married!!

RALPH: What do you mean....can't?.....we decided=======

CHERYL: You can't get married!!!!

RALPH: Sweetheart......the color thing don't matter to us.....

7 - ONE ACT PLAYS

CHERYL: Don't you understand?......it's not the color thing....something bad will happen .....

CAROL: Cheryl......please calm down......we're all adults....we don't understand.......what bad thing will happen?

CHERYL: I [HYSTERIA BUILDING]...I don't know.....damn it, I don't know........I only know something bad -------

ALEX: Baby, you're getting hysterical......maybe you should go inside and lie down......Sandy'll go with you......

CHERYL: I don't want to lie down......Alex......you must stop them......you must stop them....

CAROL: Perhaps I shouldn't be here.?......this is for you and your children......

RALPH: No......this includes us all......I don't understand Cherry.....this is not her......I know my daughter......

CAROL: But it is ---------

CHERYL: Please........everyone.....listen to me......I know I've never said anything like this before......I don't know why I'm saying it now......I don't even understand myself.....but there is something wrong with your getting married.....

RALPH: Cherry,....you're not a racist......why are you talking--------

CHERYL: [INTERRUPTING]...Will you believe?......I don't know------

RALPH: This is insane........I thought your mother and I raised a family to be open........to include everyone......

CHERYL: You did dad .....you did.....

RALPH: I remember baby......you were just a teenager when your grandfather told you his story from World War II......from when he was a soldier......and how white American soldiers died because negro American nurses were not allowed to take care of them....they could treat German wounded, but not American....how you reacted?.....at the stupidity?.....at the waste?.....you haven't changed......[CHERYL IS CRYING NOW....LOW SOBS] now everyone......I want you to pay attention......Carol and I aren't children.......this is not some wild engagement for sex...we are both well past that.......this is two people who sincerely like each other......who make each other feel warm and needed again......different from our children.....two people who want to be with each other all the time......and that, my children, ...that is as good a definition of love as any I can think of..... [AT THIS POINT CHERYL BREAKS DOWN AND RUNS TO THE BEDROOM......SANDY INDICATES, WITH HER HANDS,...THAT ALL SHOULD STAY AND SHE WILL GO TO HER....SANDY EXITS]

ALEX: [APOLOGETICALLY]...I'm sorry.....I don't understand either......she's never acted this way before.....she was happy that dad found someone to share his life.....Carol, she bragged to people about you.....to her friends....to everyone.

CAROL: Did she say I was black?

ALEX: It wasn't the first fact about you........but, she certainly didn't hide it......it can't be race.....she's never been a bigot......we have black friends and so do our kids......our house looks like the UN sometimes......

RALPH: Stanley,......did she say anything to you?

STAN: No.....whenever I spoke to her, she was happy with the arrangement.......if she was concerned about anyone, it was Carol,...and that she would be happy living in your community......

CAROL: [OBVIOUSLY UPSET]...What should we do?....should we postpone the wedding?

RALPH: [BEING VERY ASSERTIVE]..Postpone nothing.....the wedding will happen......I paid for the honeymoon already......Alex, you get your wife to a good shrink....I'll pay for it........

ALEX: You don't have to pay for anything, dad.....we'll get to the bottom of this......this is not Cherry.....there has to be an answer......a reason...

RALPH: Okay, but don't take too long.....and I don't want to hear that she hated her mother and me.....

STAN: Dad, that's a cliché.......it works in storybooks......this is real life.......Cherry was devoted to you and mom......

RALPH: All I know is, "Something's fishy in the state of Denmark.".........fix this.....I don't want Carol hurt.....

[LIGHTS DIM.....END OF SCENE]

[TWO DAYS LATER......SAME LOCATION......RALPH IS SEATED IN A COMFORTABLE CHAIR....ALEX IN ONE LESS COMFORTABLE...]

ALEX: Dad,.....I've been at her for two days......she's turning herself inside out.....she's not only pissed at herself, she's pissed at me.........can't we just put this aside?.......ignore it?....

RALPH: There's no putting aside.....I'm going to marry Carol with or without my daughter's blessing.......but that's the easy part.....what's behind this?.....this is not my daughter......not the daughter her mother and I raised.....

ALEX: I know.....I know......it makes no sense to me either....it can't be bigotry....she's been up to her behind fighting anti-Semitism and it's causes since the sixth grade......she writes....she teaches...I couldn't count how many black people have been at our table, and we at theirs.....I've been with her marching for black equality....especially in the schools......never has she done anything like this.....

RALPH: And the shrink?

ALEX: She doesn't want to talk to him......but he's our friend..I spoke to him myself.....he said it could be anything, but wouldn't possibly know without working with her......

RALPH: Maybe, she should have a quiet talk with Carol?....

ALEX: I suggested that......but she's ashamed to face her....she knows that she's wrong......but don't know why.....it's killing her as much as you.......

7 - ONE ACT PLAYS

RALPH: Well, she better get herself together.....Carol and her family will be here in a little while......I expect her to be nice.....

ALEX: She will be, dad,.....I'm sure.....

[STAN AND SANDY ENTER FROM THE KITCHEN]

SANDY: Everything's all set dad.....the little food....the big food......the champagne.......the party will be wonderful...

STAN: [INTERRUPTING] And we will have the beer.....Ying Ling........[TURNS TO ALEX] How's Cherry doing?

ALEX: I wish I could give you a definitive answer.....I don't know is probably the closest I could get......

STAN: Your buddy can't help her?

ALEX: She won't even talk to him......

STAN: Maybe I should talk to her?

ALEX: She's in the bedroom upstairs....maybe she'll open up to you......you can't make it worse.....

STAN: I'll try.......[HE EXITS UPSTAGE]

SANDY: Dad, are you hungry?...you haven't eaten since breakfast.....you don't have to wait for them to come..

RALPH: I'm not hungry.....I'm worried....

SANDY: [GOES TO HIM AND SITS ON THE ARM OF THE CHAIR]. Don't worry...somehow, it will work itself out....... Cherry will come to grips with herself......

RALPH: [HE'S CONFIDING IN SANDY....LOOKING FOR HELP]...I keep thinking.....what did I do?.....or maybe say?....in my whole life to make her be this way?........it's not from her mother....I know my children aren't perfect.....no one can be perfect.....but this?....this I don't know.....this I cannot accept....

SANDY: From what I understand, Cherry can't accept it either..... give her time.....

RALPH: But I won't stop the wedding......

SANDY: I promise....you won't have to.....[THE DOORBELL RINGS]...I'll get it......[SANDY ANSWERS THE DOOR... CAROL ENTERS WITH MELANIE].......Hi,.....come on in......Carol, [KISSING HER]..it's good to have you again........ and you, [REACHING OUT WITH BOTH HANDS].... of course, are Melanie.....welcome to our home......I'm Sandy.... [POINTING]..Alex, my brother in law....[HE NODS]....you already know Ralph.....

MELANIE: Yes, I do.....and I'm so glad to be here.....but I'm missing, I believe, Stan and Cheryl......

SANDY: Oh, there about.....coffee?

MELANIE: Sounds great....but tea, if you please......don't ask me why, but I've been on a tea binge for months....

ALEX: Better than Vodka.......

7 - ONE ACT PLAYS

MELANIE: Cheaper too....

RALPH: Why don't we all sit down?....[PEOPLE FIND CHAIRS AS HE CONTINUES]....where are Sam and the boys?

CAROL: They'll not be too long......James has a little league game and Sam's a coach......Webster's with them.....

RALPH: You'll like them, Alex......they're terrific little kids....

ALEX: Good........I'm still waiting for grandchildren......maybe they'll help to break me in......

CAROL: Break, I'm afraid, may be the right verb.....

ALEX: I can chance that....besides, it's Sandy's house......

SANDY: Thanks a lot......

MELANIE: [JOKING]..I'll have you know that they are perfectly well behaved children......and that's despite anything my mother may say......

SANDY: Sugar?

MELANIE: No......straight....thank you....

ALEX: Melanie, I see your sister on TV all the time......didn't know she was your sister until just recently.......pretty girl......but she puts herself in some awfully tough situations getting all those stories in the Middle East.......what, the devil, led her to that?

CAROL: [INTERJECTING]....You have to understand..... both my daughters are a little crazy.....Althea, she's the oldest,..... joined ROTC in college......she was an army lieutenant in the first Desert Storm.. left the service after six years and decided to become a journalist.. unfortunately, war had become her area of expertise..something that I don't understand.......Melanie, on the other hand, found romance in chemistry.....I can't understand that either......I'm praying that, at least one of the boys stays artistic..... they both show the inclination..

[STAN AND CHERYL ENTER FROM UPSTAGE]

STAN: [GOING DIRECTLY TO MELANIE] And you are Melanie....I'm Stan, the prodigal son.......in the Passover Seder, he's the wise one

MELANIE: I've been to a number of Seders.....who's the simple son?

STAN: My father's accused me of being that too......seriously, I'm so glad you're here.......but I don't see Sam and your boys....

MELANIE: Soon,....they'll show up soon....

CHERYL: [GOING TO CAROL]...Carol,....please forgive me....I don't like to think that I'm stupid or mean or anything...... but I can't seem to get beyond this strange trepidation......

CAROL: Cheryl, I can see that it's difficult......we'll find a way to overcome it.....

7 - ONE ACT PLAYS

CHERYL: [REACHING OUT HER HANDS TO MELANIE]...Melanie, I'm Cheryl .....or Cherry.....whichever works.....Sandy!...is the coffee on?

SANDY: In the carafe......help yourself......

CHERYL: Listen, everyone......I want to say something......I know you all want to talk about the wedding......I promise.....I'm cool....I'll be quiet.....

STAN: Not yet.....we'll wait for Sam.....[TONGUE IN CHEEK]...certain things are men's business.....

SANDY: You and Alex and Sam can do whatever you want....but we girls will make the important decisions......and the party..... you guys can pay for it.....

STAN: [STILL TONGUE IN CHEEK]. Already a family argument...

SANDY: All right big shot......which flowers do you think we should choose?

STAN: How would I know?......big colorful ones....

SANDY: See what I mean......okay ....go on.....with your buddies... plan away.....my hero.....

[THE DOORBELL RINGS.....STAN OPENS IT.....SAM ENTERS WITH JAMES, AGE NINE, STILL IN HIS BASEBALL CAP AND SHIRT.....WEBSTER, AGE SIX, IN PLAYGROUND CLOTHES....STAN SHAKES HANDS WITH SAM WARMLY AND SHOOS EVERYONE IN]

CAROL: Everyone.....the rest of my brood.....Sam, the coach....James, the second baseman,....and --------

WEBSTER: [INTERRUPTING......PERKY....PROUDLY....STEPPING FORWARD]....And I'm Webster, the skateboard champion.....

[CHERYL SUDDENLY COMES TO LIFE....BUT, AS IF IN A TRANCE.....SHE RUSHES TO WEBSTER.....GETS ON HER KNEES.....SHE IS CRYING AND HUGGING HIM.....THE BOY IS BEWILDERED, BUT DOESN'T BREAK AWAY. EVRYONE ELSE IS COMPLETELY DRAWN TO THE SCENE AND EQUALLY BEWILDERED]

CHERYL: Nathan!....Nathan!.....where have you been?.....I missed you......I missed you so much.....Miss. Me Graw said that you died...that you were run over by a truck....but you see....you didn't die.....you're here....with me....she wouldn't let us play together......we couldn't hold hands.....I cried.....but they wouldn't tell me where you went.......

[ALEX STEPS IN AND TAKES CHERYL FROM WEBSTER.......ALL ARE STUNNED......CHERYL IS WEEPING....WEBSTER RUNS TO HIS MOTHER, WHO TAKES HIM ASIDE......JAMES TO HIS FATHER....STAN STEPS FORWARD......ALEX HAS TAKEN CHERYL OFF STAGE]

STAN: What just happened?

SANDY: I think we're beginning to learn what has been driving Cheryl's behavior......it's got to be something terrible in her past......

STAN: But what?.........I spent my whole young life with her......I don't know......this doesn't make sense........

SANDY: It may not make sense at the moment......but, hopefully, it should start to explain things.......I'm going to her....[SHE EXITS]

STAN: This is so strange..........what could it mean?

CAROL: Let's all take a deep breath.......give them some time to calm her..........Ralph, would you find some cookies or something for the boys...........

RALPH: Sure........c'mon guys............cookies......and how would you like to play with Stan's computer?

SAM: I'll help you...........[ALL FOUR EXIT]

CAROL: Stan, any thoughts?

STAN: None of any value............

[CHERYL ENTERS......FOLLOWED BT STAN AND SANDY.......SHE GOES TO MELANIE.......CONTRITE]

CHERYL: I'm so sorry.................please everyone........forgive me........Melanie, please.........I didn't mean to upset your children........

MELANIE: [AS RALPH AND SAM REENTER]..Cheryl...... they're fine....don't worry about them...........but you........what?.......... are you okay?...

CHERYL: I'm calming down......I....I'll be all right......it's all slowly coming back to me now......I understand.....or at least I think I understand...

ALEX: Sweetheart......why don't you take a drink of water.....you'll feel better....[HE GOES FOR WATER]

CHERYL: [REGAINING COMPOSURE]....Carol.....dad.....I must apologize for all the things I've said............Carol, you're so good for dad..........and I should be so happy for you both........and, truly, I am...but when I saw Nathan.....I mean Webster.......the whole history just flooded back to me........a history, a story that I've never told anyone............not even my parents......I was so ashamed of what I thought I had done......it was my deep dark secret......so deep, that I'd forgotten it........I guess that the right word for what I'd done is...repress......that I repressed the memory......

ALEX [REENTERS WITH THE WATER]......Slow honey.....drink this.

CHERYL: [SIPPING SLOWY]...Let me start at the beginning.....I was, maybe, Webster's age.....first grade....in school.....I shared a desk with a lovely boy named Nathan.....he was black....but we liked each other, and we played with each other.....and we became best friends......so much so that we played family together....he was the father and I was the mother.....and we got married and had a bunch of imaginary children......one day, Miss. Mcgoop, or something like that.....well, she caught us holding hands....and she screamed at us that this was not allowed.......and then she separated our desks to different sides of the room......she said that children like us have to stay apart or bad things will happen.....we didn't understand her....so, when she wasn't looking, we held hands again......then, the next day, Nathan didn't come to school.......the teacher said he was run over and killed by a truck in the street......I was devastated......a bad thing happened .....my very best friend......it was my fault......and then, when I saw your Webster......I guess I flipped......or whatever word would cover my actions......

CAROL: My God.........all this time.....buried......what a horrible revelation......thank goodness, it came out......I think we're all so relieved.......to say nothing of how you feel......

CHERYL: Now, it occurs to me......what if Nathan didn't die in an accident?.....what if the teacher made it all up?

ALEX: Not now, honey......but, I promise,.....tomorrow, I'll contact some friends in the New York City school system...... we'll find out the truth.......

RALPH: Good.....you do that......and everyone, now that we've solved the great mystery.......can we get back to the question of what we're going to eat at the wedding?

[END OF PLAY]

NEW DIRECTIONS

A new one act play by Jerry "Josh" Konsker

OPENING SCENE

[THE DRIVEWAY OF A TWO CAR GARAGE IN SUBURBAN LONG ISLAND, NEW YORK. A SIGN OVER THE DOUBLE GARAGE DOOR READS; "WELCOME HOME DENNIS."

A GROUP OF VARIED PEOPLE ARE AT THE SIGHT. DENNIS KNOWS MANY WELL, OTHERS NOT SO MUCH.....ALL ARE WISHING HIM WELL.....IN THE FORE-FRONT IS DENNIS, SIX FOOT TWO INCHES TALL, AND HIS FIANCE JANET - FIVE FOOT FIVE INCHES TALL AND VERY ATTRACTIVE.

HE IS IN HIS ARMY UNIFORM WITH FIRST SERGEANT STRIPES AND A CHEST FULL OF RIBBONS PLUS A CIB.....JANET AND ALL OTHERS ARE CASUAL.]

DENNIS: Jan, it was crazy.....the whole ride from Penn station to here.....this parade of people....all wanting to shake my hand and to thank me for serving...you'd think I was a general....

JANET: That's the way people think and thank today....and no general did what you did....

DENNIS: Not true....some of them have amazing combat records....but more important...those dopey eyes of yours....the way they sparkle....they used to keep me up at night, just thinking of them....their light wouldn't let me fall off....

JANET: You use that line on all the girls?

DENNIS: I would try, but you don't get too friendly with the Arab adults....and to them...girls of thirteen are already adults......it's the kids you can win over....but it's hard....nobody really trusts anyone....

LUCY: [PUSHING EVERYONE ASIDE] As your aunt, I'm entitled to a kiss...and this time, I hope you're here to stay!! [DENNIS SMOTHERS HER]

SAM: [A FRIEND OF THE FAMILY] Denny boy, that's an impressive bunch of ribbons on your chest.....It took me three years to make it to PFC....I recognize the purple heart and the Afgan theatre of operations,... even the good conduct ribbon, I got one of those also....but what's the blue and red one?

RICK: [DENNIS' YOUNGER BROTHER AGE FIFTEEN] That's his distinguished Service Cross.....his CO put him in for the medal of honor.....my brother's a real hero, that's why they promoted him so fast....

DENNIS: Slow down Rick......no hero....they almost knocked me dead.....I was just in the wrong place at the right time.....

RICK: Bullshit....I read the citation....he exposed himself, drawing fire so the medic could get the wounded in his platoon......he

7 - ONE ACT PLAYS

knocked out a machine gun nest with grenades....I always knew my brother was an idiot.....

ANDY: [A FRIEND OF DENNIS] What happened to all that beautiful hair you were so proud of?.....now you look like all those marines on the TV shows.....

DENNIS: Tough to keep the sand out of it....most guys went bald altogether...

JANET: He promised to come home with me...can I have a turn now?

DENNIS: I'm with you sweetie, ...we have a lot to talk about and a lot of decisions to make....can we get away from here?

JANET: My apartment....and I've wanted you alone in it for a long time now.....

END OF SCENE 1

SCENE 2

[JANET'S APARTMENT....A SIMPLE LIVING ROOM... ONE COUCH, TWO CHAIRS....SOME LIGHT TABLES AND LAMPS....DENNIS IS SEATED ON THE COUCH]

DENNIS: Jan, my head is swimming.....two days ago a captain Stevenson and a master sergeant Wheeler had me in the captain's office all afternoon. ...with a few hundred arguments, they tried to get me to reenlist.....it started simply, how good a soldier I was....and that the country needed me.....first, another stripe to master sergeant.....this means nothing to me, I told them.... then an appointment to Officer's Candidate School. .....I told them that I wanted an education, but not that one....the OCS officers I served under were very unimpressive soldiers....they were going nowhere.... "But you would be," said the captain, "with your record," THEN HE UPPED THE ANTE....."The DSC and your record," the captain said slowly, "I've spoken to my CO....we could get you an appointment to West Point"....Honey, do you realize what that means?....a full scholarship, all expenses paid, to one of the most prestigious schools in the country, The GI Bill won't give us anything close to that......

JANET: I don't think you can be married if you go to West Point....

DENNIS: So we'll be married in the eyes of God or in the church...

JANET: Then what?

7 - ONE ACT PLAYS

DENNIS: A five year commitment to serve, but wives live and move with their husbands. Plus it's a fairly good income, with present and lifetime perks.

JANET [A BIT HYSTERICAL] Wives don't go with their husbands into war zones!

DENNIS: Honey, we won't always be at war....there are fine companies, all over America, who deliberately hire West Point and Annapolis graduates. Also, by the time I've completed the five years, we'd have eleven years of service in,...nine more and I'd be eligible for retirement at age forty one, with our whole lives in front of us.

JANET And children?

DENNIS: The captain has three and the sergeant two.

JANET: I'm scared....you almost got killed this time exposing yourself....even you brother called you crazy....do you like being a soldier?

DENNIS: [THINKING SLOWLY] Sometimes yes, sometimes no....I have mixed feelings....at least, I've found something I'm good at.

JANET: This is coming at me too fast. ....I really need time.....

DENNIS: Unfortunately, we haven't a lot of time.....I have only two weeks to give them my answer....they would have to make the enrollment period at the point....Also, I think we need a full family discussion with your family and mine...one way or another, they expect us to get married......I wouldn't want to disappoint them....they won't buy us just living together......

JANET: [STANDING] In the meantime....shut up and follow me in the bedroom....

[DIM LIGHTS FOR PASSAGE OF TIME ....LIGHTS UP ON THE SAME SCENE...DENNIS IS AGAIN RELAXED ON THE COUCH...JANET IS FIXING COOL DRINKS]

DENNIS: Sweetheart, I could live in your arms like that forever.....

JANET: Sounds wonderful....here...drink some lemonade... it should cool you off.....besides, your thoughts are not very realistic.....

DENNIS: Okay, ...he's realistic....there were many times, when I lay on the ground, covered with dust and sand and talking to myself, I swore, that if I make it through this in one piece, I'm going to make the rest of this life a good one....the big brass were always pulling me out to be introduced to visiting politicians.... all because of the DSC and the rank.....I made a good story.....

JANET: Of course they would...you're a very special person and you did some very special things......

DENNIS: That's the point....most of these congressmen didn't have clue as to what was going on...they got briefed by the generals....and they patted me on the back.....only one, a Vietnam veteran knew how to ask if the troops were being fed, armed, and had their backs covered....

7 - ONE ACT PLAYS

JANET: And then what?

DENNIS: You know, I've been reading a lot...I read that any great leader rarely gets more than he gives......

JANET: Don't tell me you found God?

DENNIS: Hell no....could you see me as a minister?...even your father would laugh.....One chaplain gave me a lot of philosophy to read...he didn't get to me for religion....besides, he was Jewish.....something else is, and I can't explain it.....

JANET: Is this the same person that I haven't seen in close to a year?....It's not that I can see that....I can feel that.....I don't love him less....does he love me less?

DENNIS: Oh God no,.....I love you more....I can't think of doing anything in this life without you beside me.....

JANET: This is beginning to feel like the start of a bad movie....

DENNIS: Okay, let's try to examine this slowly and clearly....if we both want to make something worthwhile with of our lives....we need better educations.......West Point for me, has to be an option....lack of money or other resources probably means a community or local college for you.....

JANET: [EXPLODING] But that separates us.....

DENNIS: Not really.....West point is only two hours away by car....I couldn't see you during the week anyway...many weekends, you could come to me.....

JANET: Denny, you've given this a lot more thought than you led me to believe....Dennis, whatever is in your mind is driving these decisions....Do you like being a soldier? Or is it something else?

DENNIS: Honey, I'm not a warrior....but I have become a fighter...and I'm willing to bust my ass for the right goal....I think that soldiering could be the best path for us.....almost all the congressmen and dignitaries that I've met don't impress me other than they all are educated...we should be among them....I also want to help guide this country from an experience that lawyers and fat cats can't understand.....

JANET: Even without an education, I know that these fat cats have alt the money....

DENNIS: I already have the medal....without that and the point, I could never be a bird colonel or general....I could even write a book....it would take that kind of prestige and history....

JANET: But the army teaches you to shoot people, not to talk to them......

DENNIS: Not true....only a small, very small part of the army is only concerned with shooting people....the degree in West Point could be in history, or political science, or even geography....I could aim for assignments in our embassies or in teaching....with posts like that, we can always be together and able to raise a family......

JANET: You never had more than a C plus average in high school, now you're a statesman and a professor?

DENNIS: I've matured a bit...I'm healthy and strong and athletic....I'll need that as part of the education....also, I won't skip classes any longer.....

DIM LIGHT END OF SCENE

SCENE 4

[THE LIVING ROOM OF DENNIS' PARENTS...JOHN AND LYDDY LAUGHTEN...JOHN IS SEATED IN A LARGE CHAIR...LYDDY AND DENNIS ARE STANDING NEARBY]

JOHN Let me get this straight son,....you didn't have enough?.....that medal doesn't mean shit to your mom and me.....we're just happy you're here.....now you want more?....an entire career of it? what is the mortality of lieutenants in the com bat zone?....I'm sure it's easier to count those still alive......

DENNIS: Dad, please....you're oversimplifying everything......that's not all there is to do in the service....we won't always be at war.....and with my record, I'll be a captain in two years...

[THE DOORBELL RINGS....AS DENNIS ANSWERS THE DOOR, JANET ENTERS WITH HER PARENTS BILL AND ALICE TRAST....THE FAMILIES ARE COMFORTABLE WITH EACH OTHER...KISSES AND HUGS, ETC.]

BILL: John, do you realize what these two idiot kids want to do?....Now, I can't give Dennis a vice presidency in the firm where I work, but I can think of a whole lot of futures for them other than what they are talking about.....

LYDDY: Let's hear them out.....if you can't dream in your twenties, when will you ever do it?....this is not Bonnie and Clyde....this is Janet and Dennis......

JOHN: All right, fair enough, why don't you guys start at the beginning?

7 - ONE ACT PLAYS

DENNIS: [STEPPING UP] The beginning is to establish the things we can all agree upon.....first and foremost......Jan and I have waited two long years for each other.....no matter how we struggle, we want to do it together.....so we're going to marry as soon as it can be arranged.....

BILL: Hear....hear.....

DENNIS: Second....we both want a college education....there isn't much money in either family and we have siblings......we can do it on our own....we're offered two paths....me, a West Point scholarship, probably worth about half million dollars....Janet, the harder way, some work and community colleges....I've put together a few thousand dollars army pay, so that's a good head start.....What ever she hasn't completed after my four years at the point, she would complete, wherever we are, as an army wife at vastly reduced costs......

JANET: Than, depending on Dennis' assignment, we can start a family, two boys and two girls, one named for each of you....

ALICE: You're guaranteeing an even split?

JANET: Of course.....the four is easy...we may have to stretch the naming a little bit......

DENNIS: These are the mechanical things....the next may be harder to fathom......I've tried to explain it to Jan, and I doubt that I've fully succeeded....

JANET: I understand you better than you think I do....

DENNIS: I sure hope so sweetheart.....neither of our families are especially religious.....now, I haven't found God, as the born again Christians say they do.....but I have found Dennis....and I've done a lot of reading....When I was recovering in the hospital in Manheim, a chaplain or a field grade officer, I'm not sure which, sat down at my bed.....he asked, "When we do as you have done, do we serve a greater God? Or perhaps this. Our country, when it's at it's best, are they equal? Or are they one in the same?" That's a hell of a question. One could take a lifetime finding an answer. Another thing got me while attending the funeral for some of the guys in my company. The minister quoted a psalm, it said, "Those that wait upon the lord, shall renew their strength....they shall mount up with wings as eagles, they shall run and not be weary." ......Folks, my inspiration comes when I switch the word man for Lord......

BILL: That's quite a mouthful Den....if you talk like that, you could be a minister....but you've certainly matured.....

DENNIS: That's part of the project, but the secular one.....

JOHN: Sounds to me that you two have pretty much made up your minds. If so, what do you do next? And what can we do to help you?

BILL: Right on John, ...kids, we can't and won't stand in your way.....

ALICE: I still don't like all this army business....

LYDDY: Jan, that means a lot more time at home with me...

7 - ONE ACT PLAYS

JANET: Mom, not much different than the last two years.... except, now you and Mrs Laughton must plan a simple wedding.... maybe on our back lawn....no more than six thousand people.....

DENNIS: Remember, I'm still in uniform and a first sergeant. I've got to tell Captain Stevenson that I would like to go to West Point...Also, I have three weeks leave still do me...If they'll give me the money, I'll grab it and add it to Jan's college fund.. Otherwise, Jan and I will be forced to spend all that time at some resort somewhere..I hear they give very special deals to veterans and soldiers in uniform. Oh yes there is something you can do for me. I'd like to borrow your car for some time..Another thing to understand, I will try for a degree in history at the Point..if I get it, I might be able to teach at the army war college..and later, at a university after I retire from the service, or else think about Running for congress.

BILL Why not run for president?

DENNIS: I'll do that after six years in the legislature.

DIM LIGHTS
END OF PLAY

www.ingramcontent.com/pod-product-compliance
Lightning Source LLC
LaVergne TN
LVHW011936070526
838202LV00054B/4672